A green laser swept across the room and landed on Sasha's chest.

Judah's heart raced and he shoved her into the shadows, then dived onto the bed, covering Bodie with his body. The child screamed and squirmed beneath him as gunfire sprayed through the room. Glass shattered and debris pelted his back as he pulled Bodie to the floor.

Sasha crawled over, grabbed her gun again, then reached for Bodie. "It's okay, baby. I'm here."

The little boy lunged for his mother, who pulled him into the bathroom. Judah followed and closed the door.

"Guess they found me." Sasha hugged her son tight with one hand, her weapon in the other.

"It's not like we had you well hidden. We've got to move. What's the best way out?"

"There isn't one." Sasha looked back into the room and more gunfire erupted. She pulled in tight next to him, her body trembling against his. "This place isn't like the Whitmore property. There's no secret way out or panic rooms. We're gonna have to fight."

Shannon Redmon remembers the first grown-up book she checked out from the neighborhood bookmobile. A Victoria Holt novel, with romance, intrigue and ballroom parties, captivated her attention and flamed her desire to write. She hopes her stories immerse readers in a world of joy and escape while encouraging faith, hope and love for those around us. Shannon is represented by Tamela Hancock Murray of the Steve Laube Agency.

Books by Shannon Redmon

Love Inspired Suspense

Cave of Secrets
Secrets Left Behind
Mistaken Mountain Abduction
Christmas Murder Cover-Up
Unraveling Killer Secrets

Visit the Author Profile page at LoveInspired.com.

Unraveling Killer Secrets

SHANNON REDMON

LOVE INSPIRED SUSPENSE
INSPIRATIONAL ROMANCE

LOVE INSPIRED® SUSPENSE
INSPIRATIONAL ROMANCE

ISBN-13: 978-1-335-98011-3

Unraveling Killer Secrets

Copyright © 2024 by Shannon Moore Redmon

Recycling programs
for this product may
not exist in your area.

Love Inspired
22 Adelaide St. West, 41st Floor
Toronto, Ontario M5H 4E3, Canada
www.LoveInspired.com

Printed in Lithuania

MIX
Paper | Supporting
responsible forestry
FSC® C021394

And be ye kind one to another, tenderhearted,
forgiving one another, even as God for Christ's sake
hath forgiven you.
—*Ephesians* 4:32

To my family, the Redmons,
who have always supported my writing
and books. I couldn't have done this without
all your encouragement. I love you.

ONE

Hank Adler was dead. Murdered. One fatal bullet to the chest.

Forensic photographer Sasha Kane stood over the man's body and aimed her camera lens at his face—ash-colored skin, dark hair slicked back from bushy brows and disturbing eyes still open with the same vacant stare she witnessed in every murder victim's photo, but this was different. Hank was her friend, and his death was personal. The familiar burn of grief tightened her chest and blurred her vision, but she fought back her emotions, determined not to contaminate the crime scene.

She worked quickly, before the sun faded outside the large floor-to-ceiling windows and robbed her of its natural warmth and glow. Eerie shadows stretched across the waiting room decorated with leather couches, fine art and Turkish rugs that cushioned the hardwood floors. Only the finest for Hank.

Sasha lowered her camera's f-stop to capture more light, then moved through her mental checklist to make sure she didn't miss any details that might help find his killer.

She stepped back to the office door. To the left, shattered glass from a broken lamp and two framed diplomas littered the floor next to his body. Blood spatter covered the manila folders stacked on his desk and dotted the wall at chest height. A bullet, piercing the plaster, left a round dark hole in the middle of the red pattern. Crime scene investigators would dig out the evidence and log it in their database. She prayed something here would be a match to whoever committed this heinous crime.

Sasha moved closer to Hank's desk. Among the folders was one with her name on the tab, lying open for all who entered to see. Red droplets spattered the pages and blotted out most of the information. Hopefully enough to keep her secret. More hot tears rushed to her eyes, and she swiped them away. This was not the time to break down. She had to be strong and finish her job.

Something thumped against the wall. Sasha spun toward the noise.

No one was there.

A beep from a car echoed outside, and headlights flashed through the window. She separated the blinds and peeked out. Mr. Bell, the store manager from downstairs, locked his coffee shop door and drove off, oblivious to the crime above him. Sasha noted the time, his tag number and the make of his car to add to the report for the investigators. Everything had to be recorded, no matter how insignificant a detail might seem. The timeline was most important in a murder case, although she doubted Mr. Bell, who'd always been nice to her by providing free coffees in exchange for comped marketing photos, had anything to do with the harm that Hank endured. Only an evil person filled with hatred could carry out such a violent act, and Mr. Bell wasn't that kind of man.

She raised her camera again and snapped a few more shots. Hank's office wasn't large, but the prime location, at the corner of Main Street and Fourth Avenue, had its perks. Since he was positioned above the Bean Stalk, the entire space smelled of espresso and frothed milk. One of the reasons Hank had bought the building.

All kinds of professional types frequented the shop during the day, but at this time of night Mr. Bell went home to his family and closed up by 7:00 p.m. Some of the neighboring restaurants and bars kept their door open to let in the cooler, evening air. Even summers in the mountains had their hot temperatures and she hoped a witness might've heard or seen something that would help identify Hank's killer.

If only she'd come to their meeting sooner, Hank might still be alive, helping her navigate all the legal documents he'd put together for her.

She pressed her shutter button again—*click*.

Or two bodies would've ended up in bags tonight and her son would be without a mother.

She shuddered at the thought and hoped the crime scene investigators would get here soon. When she'd radioed dispatch earlier, they'd told her units were on their way, but no sirens cut through the quiet town. Not yet anyway.

Another thump sounded to her right. She straightened and turned toward the door. Sasha moved around her friend's body, looked out into the lobby and scanned the space.

"Hello?"

No one answered.

The old building creaked a little but having been built in the 1930s with the basement acting as the town's only bomb shelter during World War II, she figured that was normal. Maybe she was imagining things, or someone had thumped the wall in the office next door. The room turned quiet again as Sasha settled back into a rhythm of clicks, taking more photos.

She stepped in front of a small closet bordered by built-in bookcases and crouched for a close-up of Hank's hands. A number was written on his left palm. Six digits. Too short to be a phone number. Maybe a combination to a locker or something. She snapped a picture.

The floor creaked, and she stood again, chills radiating up her arms. Sasha wasn't imagining things. The noises were coming from inside the office. She wasn't alone.

Metal scraped behind her. With her camera lowered, resting against her abdomen, she turned.

The closet door stood open and a shadow moved inside.

Sasha bolted for the door. From her peripheral vision, a man lunged from the darkness, shoving her into the wall. She turned, his breath hot in her face. With a quick defense move, she slammed her elbow into his jaw, but he didn't flinch.

Instead, his muscular arm landed across her chest and pressed into her throat. She fought to breathe, then stilled, hoping he'd loosen the pressure. By pretending to be cooperative, she might gain another chance to break free.

She raised her gaze to his. Excitement flashed in his black eyes.

"Give me the camera." His voice was low, deep with a slight lisp when he spoke.

"If you want my photos, you have to loosen your grip so I can get the strap from around my neck."

He hesitated then straightened, removing his crushing weight from her small frame. Sasha dipped her head and grasped the long telephoto lens. This was the only opportunity she might have to escape.

With a quick movement, she swung the device as hard

as possible, striking his temple and knocking him back. Blood trickled from the gash, and he swiped the cut with his finger, then grabbed for the telephoto lens, pulling her along with the device.

Sasha leaned back, the strap still secured around her neck, and tightened her grip. With the lens aimed upward, she snapped a flash photo of his face. The bright light triggered dots in her vision, but instead of recoiling, the man gripped the strap tighter and twisted it around her throat. His dark eyes flared and his sharp jaw tightened, exaggerating the small scar on his left cheek. A gang tattoo flexed on his right forearm.

She scratched at the fabric with her fingers, unable to create any space underneath. Her lungs burned, and white dots along the edges of her vision turned to black. If she didn't fight, the investigators would find her dead body right beside Hank's.

Sasha punched her boot heel into the man's knee. He stumbled, releasing his grip, and she was able to break free, gasping for air. Sirens echoed closer, and her attacker reversed course, making a run for the window.

Adrenaline pumped through every muscle in her body. She was a fighter and wanted this guy to pay for her friend's death. Sasha shot up, rounded desks and jumped over potted plants, determined to snap as many photos as possible. Mostly of his back, but every bit of evidence helped.

Metal clanged when he landed on the fire escape outside and disappeared from her view. She rushed to the second-story window, aiming her lens in his direction. He jumped to the ground, then, with one glance back up, made a mistake. Sasha caught the fullness of his face and clicked. Dark eyes narrowed in her direction, and his black goatee outlined the sneer on his face.

He jerked down the bill of his ratty ball cap. "You'll regret that."

He ran toward the parking garage at the bottom of the hill, his black biker boots echoing off the concrete when he disappeared inside.

More footsteps thumped into the room behind her. "Shadow Creek Police."

She turned to the door with her hands raised. "He went—"

Officers filled the room, but Sasha's gaze fell to one man.

Detective Judah Walker stood before her with his gun aimed at her chest. His tall frame hovered over the waiting room chairs, and his wavy dark hair accentuated blue eyes, piercing her heart right back into the memories of the night they'd spent together. A night that had changed her life forever. He didn't know her secret. Not yet, anyway, and now wasn't really the time to bring up their past, but she had to tell him he was her son's father. If she didn't, he'd see the custody agreement Hank put together for her. She'd kept her pregnancy and the birth of her baby hidden from him for three years. Not because he was a bad man, but they'd broken up and she'd moved away. The plan had been to tell him tonight with Hank as her mediator, but now her friend's death had changed everything. How could she ever find the courage to spill the news without Hank there to soften the blow?

Life was different now. The birth of her son had changed her. In the midst of all the uncertainty, she had surrendered her life to Jesus. She wasn't sure Judah would understand. He'd never been one to go to church or talk about spiritual issues when they dated but then again neither had she. Now, she couldn't imagine living her life without God. He'd given her the most precious gift in her sweet son, and no matter what the future held with Judah—if anything at all—he still had a right to know he was a father. Just not tonight.

Heat rushed to her cheeks as he crossed the hardwood floors towards her. Every memory and every heartache rushed to the forefront of her mind.

The awkward silence thickened between them, and she began rethinking every decision she'd made. Maybe moving home hadn't been the best idea. In Raleigh, she'd had a decent job and lived in a good neighborhood, but her family was here in the small mountain town of Shadow Creek, North Carolina, and she'd wanted to be near them.

With Judah standing in front of her, their past sins seemed too great. The last thing she wanted to do was face the consequences of their impetuous decisions, which now seemed insurmountable, but if she didn't tell him the truth, how could she ever be honest with her son?

Judah's son.

Would he forgive her for keeping such a secret from him?

She glanced back into Hank's office. The custody agreement sat right on top of the folders. Judah was sure to see them. If only they were underneath and out of plain view but they were evidence. Her secret would be entered into the police database. Once read, he would know why she'd stayed away from Shadow Creek. His life would change forever. Or worse…it wouldn't.

She motioned toward the window. "Our suspect took the fire escape to the street."

The words she wanted to say stuck inside her. She swallowed and collected all the courage she could, but it wasn't enough. Not yet. They'd lost their childhood friend tonight. Wasn't that the more pressing matter?

"What happened?" He kept his distance and pulled out his notepad to take her statement. She hesitated, weighing the words in her mind. He was here, standing in front of her. The speech she'd planned perched on the tip of her tongue. She started to speak, but the right words didn't come.

"Hank Adler's dead."

Judah holstered his gun while the other investigators cleared the room. Sasha Kane, his ex-fiancée, stood next to the windows with a camera in hand, red striations around her neck and a purple bruise on the side of her cheek. He was thankful she'd managed to survive but her revelation about his friend cut through to his gut.

She pushed her long dark hair behind her shoulder and nodded toward Hank's office door. "Did you hear me?"

He didn't want to believe her words. Hank couldn't be dead. They'd been inseparable since grade school, and Judah couldn't imagine his life without the one person who'd supported him when no one else did. "Are you sure?"

"Yeah. His body's in there."

He looked past her shoulder into the office but didn't move. As soon as he entered and saw his friend's remains, the grief would hit. Classic denial, but it was the only way he could process the news while standing in front of the only woman he'd ever loved. He glanced at the bloodstains on her shirt. "Are you hurt?"

Her fingers moved to her throat. The marks grew darker with every passing minute. "I'm fine."

"I can have the paramedic take a look at you, if—"

"Really. I'm fine."

"But the blood—"

"It's Hank's."

Another blow chipped away at his obvious delay from entering the room. "Oh."

Sasha folded her arms across her chest and let her green-eyed gaze drop to the floor. They never were good at talking about the hard times life tossed their way. When Sasha faced pain, emotional or physical, she always retreated and wanted to be alone. He liked to face their problems head-on, the sooner the better, but when rebuffed he turned to his old vice, alcohol. At least he did before Hank helped him sober up.

Judah let the matter drop, since he wasn't her fiancé anymore. She was a grown woman and could make her own health decisions, like the choice she'd made three years ago to leave him without a word.

He scanned the waiting area. Not much seemed out of place here. Maybe a magazine or two wasn't in the right spot, but everything else seemed fine, except for the open window where their suspect had escaped.

Sasha turned her camera for him to see. "Here's some photos. They might be blurry, but they'll provide some context to what happened after I arrived."

"Did you get a photo of the murderer?"

"A blurry one when he went out the window. He looked back up at me, but since I was chasing him, there's motion on the photo."

"You chased him?" He pointed at her neck. "After he almost killed you?"

She stared at him for an extra moment, as if she was surprised by his question. Sasha never was one to back down from a fight, no matter how outmatched she was. "I couldn't let him get away. Not after what he did to Hank."

Judah didn't know whether to be impressed or angry at her impulsive decision. "These photos ought to make you popular with our killer."

"Tell me about it."

Judah advanced through the images. They were blurry, yes, but a couple of them could be used. However, if they wanted a good identification that would stand up in court, he'd need Sasha to select their killer from a lineup and be willing to take the stand. Defense attorneys would shred most of these pictures with one look. "Did you see which way he went?"

"Into the parking structure underneath the building."

He motioned for a couple of patrol officers to check out the garage, then shifted his gaze to the open door of his friend's office. This was the part he always dreaded. Even though he saw dead bodies on a regular basis, the initial viewing took his breath—and this time his best friend was the victim. "He's in there, you said?"

"Yeah." She stepped to the side to let him pass. "I found him on the floor and moved in to help, but he was already gone. Then I called dispatch and started documenting the scene. After I took a few photos, the killer lunged from the closet and attacked me."

Judah jotted down a few notes. "Do you think you could ID the person who attacked you?"

"Maybe. The office was dark. We were fighting, and then he ran. Everything happened so fast, but I did get a pretty good look at him."

"I'll get a sketch artist in here and let you work with them." He was stalling. As soon as he saw his friend's body, Hank would no longer be a part of his everyday life.

The reality was almost too much to bear, but he had a job to do, and if anyone could get justice for Hank, he would.

Judah stepped through the office door, the metallic scent of death assaulting his senses. Hank's Italian-leather loafers protruded from the side of his desk. Blood was spattered on the walls and across several stacks of folders. His friend had put up a fight, judging from all the broken glass and disarray inside the room. He hoped the killer had gotten the beating he deserved. If only Hank had been the victor.

Judah knelt by his best friend's side. His chest ached with the loss. He'd tried to warn Hank about some of the clients he defended, but his friend only listened to one voice. His own. The same stubborn tenacity that worked for him in the courtroom was most likely what got him killed.

He fought back his emotions, not wanting Sasha to see him cry. "Did the killer have any tattoos, markings?"

"One on his right forearm and a scar on his left cheek. Looked like an NX5 gang tattoo."

His body tensed. NX5 gang members claimed Shadow Creek as their territory and often slipped through the legal system, courtesy of Hank's brilliant legal mind, but his friend had recently lost one of their latest cases, and a high-level NX5 member had gone to prison as a result. The man only made it one week in general population before he was fatally shanked.

A couple of weeks prior, Hank had come to Judah, worried about his safety, but no clear threat had been made against him. Judah had done everything he could to protect his friend, but having a patrol officer drive by his office and home during each shift wasn't going to stop these guys from enacting revenge for not winning the case.

"Did you take photos of Hank's body?"

"I documented everything."

He stood and held out his hand. "I'll need the SD card. The images are evidence, and I want them secured."

"I'm happy to give you a copy, but I've had too many SD cards get lost in evidence lockers, and sometimes the DA comes to me for the images."

"It's protocol." He met her gaze. Despite the obvious attack, she still looked the same after three years—the same beautiful green-eyed girl who broke his heart. Her return to his life only intensified the sting of betrayal he'd felt after she disappeared without a word.

No explanation.

No phone call.

Not even a Dear John letter.

He couldn't trust her, not then and not now.

Sasha reached into her bag, pulled out a business card and pen, then wrote something on the back, sliding the information into his hand. "The images automatically upload to a cloud account. Here's the login information. It's easiest to access the photos from there."

She let her fingers linger against his palm a moment longer than normal. "Do me one favor."

Her dark red nails dug into the skin of his hand just a bit before he pulled away. "I'm not much for professional favors. Clouds a cop's judgment."

She shook her head. "Oh, it's nothing like that. The images you'll need are in a folder labeled 'Forensic Photos.' When I get time, I'll move them into one with a specific case-file number. It's my system to keep things organized. Please keep them in the folder and don't move or delete them."

Judah flipped the business card over and read her writing on the back before looking at the front. Her name was embossed in gold with her job title underneath. "You're the department's new forensic photographer?"

"Started last week. I was in training most of that time, so unfortunately, this is my first official case. Why did you think I was taking photos?"

"I heard you did forensic photography in Raleigh, and I figured that carried over here but I didn't realize you worked for the precinct now."

"I was part of the homicide investigative team there and took all the crime scene photos. I really enjoyed it but I'm a cop first. Of course, you know that since we graduated from the police academy together. How'd you hear about my forensic photography?"

Heat flushed to his face. "Small town. People talk."

"Right."

He stood, pulled on a pair of gloves and inspected the bullet in the wall. The sooner this topic ended, the better. He didn't want her to know he'd kept tabs on her over the past few years and prayed she bought his explanation. Judah refocused on the scene in order to keep from saying something more he might regret.

"No murder weapon?"

"I didn't see one."

"Not even on the man who attacked you?"

"He didn't have one. At least not in his hand. Maybe on his person somewhere, but he never pulled it out."

"That's odd. You think he would've shot you like Hank."

"Glad he didn't."

"Or he's not our killer."

"Why else would he be here?"

"Point taken. Maybe the gun is here somewhere and he wasn't able to get to it after you arrived."

"He lunged at me from the closet."

Judah checked the small space and shelf above but found no weapon.

Another patrol officer walked over. "Detective Walker, the investigative team is here."

"Great. Let's extend the perimeter to a one-block radius and lock down the area, including the parking garage. Also, did we get a report back from the team I sent to check out that location? I need to know if they found the murder weapon."

"Nope. No murder weapon or suspect. Looks like they fled."

Judah jotted down notes and glanced at Sasha again. "And you didn't see any vehicle leave the structure, correct?"

"Not while I was at the window. Although I did see Mr. Bell leave."

"The coffee shop owner?"

"Yeah. Looked like he was locking up for the night. Nothing too suspicious, but I did get some photos of his vehicle and tag."

"Did he leave before or after you were attacked?"

"Before."

Judah added the information to his timeline. "Have you finished documenting the scene?"

"I think I've got all the required photos, plus a few extra I like to include, so I'm done here unless you need me for something else."

He'd needed her when his life was in shambles. When he hit rock bottom and thought he'd lost everything, including her. He'd never expected to hear from her again, but then she'd reached out and asked to meet tonight. "I've got a few minutes to talk if you want."

"About what?" She flipped through the photos on her

camera, then pulled a white cloth from her bag to wipe down the lens.

"Whatever you wanted to meet about today."

Sasha stopped wiping and slowly lowered her camera into the padded compartment of her bag. "This really isn't the time, not with what's happened to Hank. We can find another day to discuss a few things."

She zipped up her bag and headed for the door, but Judah followed. He knew something was up. She always bolted when she didn't want to face a difficult subject. When they'd fought about his drinking, she'd hit him with a few stinging remarks and then head for home or to a friend's house without giving them time to work through their issues.

He stepped into the hallway. "Wait a minute."

She slowed at the top of the stairs and placed a hand on the baluster. "I've really got to get going."

He walked over to her and kept his voice low. "We haven't talked in years, and out of the blue you contact me about meeting at Hank's office and then I get called to his murder scene where you're the eyewitness. What's going on? Don't you think you owe me some kind of explanation after all this time?"

"You're right. You at least deserve that, but this conversation really needs to wait until another day. With Hank's death, we need to focus on his case right now."

"Was there something going on with you and Hank?"

Her eyes widened at his implied accusation. "Nothing more than a friend helping a friend."

"Then what? Did you and Hank get in a fight or something? You were the one to discover his body. You're the one with blood on your clothes. If something happened between the two of you and things got out of hand, you can tell me. I can help find you a good lawyer."

Her body stiffened. "You can't possibly think—"

He folded his arms across his chest. "I'm not saying you pulled the trigger—"

"Are you serious? You actually think I have it in me to kill Hank? I know it's been a few years, Judah, but I would never do anything to hurt him—or anyone, for that matter. He was my good friend, too."

He hated to press, but he had to make sure she was telling him the truth. With three years gone by and the fact she was clearly hiding something from him, maybe she'd changed from the woman he knew. "Sometimes things happen. Tempers flare and—"

"I didn't shoot Hank." She paused as another officer climbed to the top of the stairs and passed them. "I can't believe you would even think something like that, especially since you know me so well. What we have to discuss has nothing to do with the case other than it is the reason I was at Hank's office in the first place."

"And why were you here? At the very time Hank was killed. Maybe I could understand better if you told me the reason."

She adjusted the camera strap on her shoulder and looked at the door. "He was helping me with a legal matter, that's all."

She headed down the stairs, out of the building and let the metal door slam behind her. Always running. That's what she did when things got tough. How would he ever be able to work with her again with so much baggage between them?

He'd focus on finding Hank's killer and then look for another job. This time he'd be the one to leave before Sasha Kane had a chance to destroy his life again.

TWO

Judah pushed open the old building's door with a creak and headed to his car, thoughts fully on his best friend. News of Hank's murder had already spread to the press, and journalists were lined up across the street snapping photos and tossing out questions to anyone who entered or exited the building. He ignored them. The last thing he wanted to do was comment on his best friend's homicide.

Camera flashes mixed with blue lights from the patrol cars stationed at both ends of the street to keep the curious crowds at bay. He scanned one group huddled off to the side—grown, tattooed men, all known to be members of NX5.

He slipped into the quiet interior of his unmarked SUV and let the day sink over him. He didn't want to forget any details and began replaying the entire scenario in his head. From his arrival to encountering Sasha, seeing Hank's body and trying to make sense of the folder opened on Hank's desk. The documents referred to Sasha and included his name, but from the blood and a large cup of coffee spilled in the struggle, he couldn't make out the purpose of Sasha's legal issue.

He rubbed his face, trying to make some sense of the entire ordeal, but the whole experience had drained him.

Maybe she was suing him over the property they'd purchased together when they were engaged. The two acres outside of town had the most beautiful mountain views and a remodeled barn where they'd planned to have their wedding. He'd not done anything with the land since she left—in fact, he'd avoided the place that held too many regrets. But for some reason he couldn't put it up for sale.

Neon tavern lights flickered at the end of a block and past addictions tempted him to enter. What he wouldn't give right now to wash away all his problems with the smooth tilt of a shot glass but alcohol only destroyed his life before and he refused to allow the poisonous hook to sink into him again.

What started off as a few drinks always turned into more—a vice he couldn't control. If only he had never started but every time his parents fought back in the day, he'd drown the soundtrack of their turmoil in a bottle of whiskey pulled from his teenage closet. He told himself he could stop, but when his mom passed away from cancer, he didn't want the numbed feeling to end. His whole world had fallen apart, and alcohol became his only constant— the one thing that brought him comfort, until it didn't.

If not for Hank's intervention during the most vulnerable time in his life, he'd still be in shambles. He refused to dishonor his friend's memory.

Judah powered up his laptop, typed the details of his initial report and tried to make sense of who might've wanted to harm his friend. He needed to go through Hank's case files to know where to begin. Maybe Hank also had a digital file of Sasha's documents and he could get more clarity about her intentions. He'd have to work fast, before his sergeant discovered the identity of their victim's body and pulled Judah from the case.

Sergeant Quinn didn't like detectives to have close ties to the homicide cases they were investigating. Judah doubted any convincing argument would sway the man, but he had to try. Hank was the closest person he had to family, the brother he always wanted, and he'd do whatever he could to bring his killer to justice.

Sasha's eyewitness account of an NX5 member at the crime scene, backed up with images, pointed at the most dangerous and active gang in the area. But she hadn't seen the man pull the trigger, and the absence of the murder weapon made the crime harder to prove.

Judah clicked through the client list he'd downloaded from Hank's computer. Any of the hundreds of names listed had motive to take his friend out, and if Hank hadn't called him a week ago asking for protection, then he might consider any one of them.

But it was Coby Evans, leader of NX5, who'd threatened his friend on the street the same night he called, leaving Hank in a bruised heap with three broken ribs. Judah had never seen his friend so scared when he found him and took him to the hospital. Hank believed they would kill him after he lost one of their high-level members cases. It looked like Coby had carried through on his promise— Judah would make sure he spent the rest of his life behind bars.

A knock on his car window broke his concentration. Sasha stood outside his door, and he rolled down the glass.

"Sorry to bother you." She tilted her head and leaned forward. "I started to leave but remembered something my attacker said."

"Shoot." He kept typing up the initial report.

"He threatened me, but I doubt he'll follow through, right?"

Judah stopped typing. "What did he say?"

"That I'd regret taking the photo of him."

"Did he mention coming back for you or harming you in any way?"

"No. Nothing like that. Do you think he was just shooting off his mouth in the heat of the moment, angry that I got a photo of him?"

"I think we have to take every threat seriously, especially if you're right and he's inked with the NX5 member tattoo. If he's guilty and thinks you can ID him, then your life is in danger. Do you have an image of the tattoo you mentioned?"

"Yeah." She retrieved her camera, clicked through to the images and handed him the device. The tattoo on the man's forearm filled the screen. "Looks like NX5 to me, but I've been gone for a while, so I wasn't sure."

Judah's chest tightened. He'd seen the familiar design way too many times in multiple crimes he'd worked. "He's definitely NX5. For these guys to even get that tattoo, they have to prove their loyalty by killing someone random."

"Do you think that's what happened to Hank? Just some random act of violence?"

He logged into the criminal database, sorted the images by identifiers and typed in left cheek scar. "I think whoever killed Hank had a motive, but we can't rule anything out yet. Hank had way too many enemies to count. Defending criminals didn't make him the most popular person in the state."

"I guess not."

Two men's pictures popped up, and he turned the screen so she could see. "Do either of these guys look familiar?"

"The one on the left."

"Well, he's not a newbie and falls in line with previous events."

"Who is he?"

Judah stepped out of his car, closed the driver's door and leaned against it. "His name is Coby Evans, and he's the leader of NX5. A week ago, Hank called me for help. I found him bruised up from a beatdown with three broken ribs. Coby had paid him a visit. The man wasn't happy with the case Hank lost. We provided some security measures but Coby is extremely slippery and dangerous. He'll not only come for you but also your family. You and your sisters need to stay somewhere safe until we arrest him."

"I'm staying at my mom's. I don't want to put her or—" She hesitated a moment, which he thought was odd.

"Or what?"

"I don't want to put my sisters in danger."

"Maybe you can go back to your aunt's. Evans doesn't have any ties to Raleigh, and you being there seemed to work before."

Her gaze dropped to the street. He hadn't meant for his statement to wound, but the words had come out a little harsher than normal. "Sorry. I shouldn't—"

"No. It's okay. You make a fair point, but my aunt isn't in good health and plans to come live with Mom, too, as soon as her house sells."

"Looks like we're stuck with you, then." He paused. "Sorry. That didn't come out right, either."

He really needed to stop with the small talk and figure out a way to keep Sasha safe.

She pushed her hands into her pockets and glanced up the street. "I better call my family. Let them know what's going on."

"With four sisters in law enforcement, I'm surprised your phone isn't ringing right now."

She pulled the device from her pocket and tapped the screen. "It's been on silent, and I already have fifteen messages from my sisters." She shifted her weight and seemed to hesitate, almost as if there was more she wanted to say. He'd interrogated enough people to know when someone was hiding something, and Sasha's behavior fit the bill, but he didn't have time for guessing games. He had an investigation to oversee. At least until his sergeant arrived.

"Guess I better go," Sasha said, but she continued to stand there.

Time to put an end to the current awkwardness. "I need to check out the parking garage and get a copy of their security footage. Maybe the cameras caught our suspect in a frame or two."

"Mind if I come along?"

He hesitated. "I thought you had to get home to talk to your sisters?"

"And as soon as I walk through the door, I'll be inundated with a bazillion questions. I don't think I'm ready for that. Besides, with most of the team here, I should be here, too. I know I'm new to the department, but I'm good at my job and I want to help."

She motioned to the growing crowd around the crime scene border. "In fact, it looks like most of the town's here. Our killer could be present, and when you get the footage, we can see if he came back. Or I can go with you. Two sets of eyes are better than one."

He held up his hand. "I'm not trying to be rude, but I could use a minute or two alone to process everything. Hank was my best friend and—"

"Say no more." She adjusted her camera strap. "I'll get

photos of the crowd while you go to the garage. We can talk later."

She walked away and remained in the shadows, aiming and snapping images of the people surrounding the street. He hadn't meant to be abrupt but having her around made his emotions about Hank's death even harder. The three of them had been inseparable growing up; they'd spent countless hours together. Judah pressed up from his car, rounded the corner of the building and leaned against the cool brick wall, forcing himself to breathe.

His best friend since childhood was dead. Hank Adler had picked him up so many times back in the day, never passing judgment but always offering his help. The man had worked wonders on his behalf, and his loyalty had never wavered while Judah figured out rehab. They'd celebrated his one year of sobriety just last week, and he wouldn't have wanted anyone else there besides Hank.

The door to a tavern across the street squeaked open. Judah straightened. If his mother were here, she would've toasted Hank's life with more than enough drinks for the two of them. In the end, liver cancer took her life, and he refused to go out in such a painful way. A relapse would be challenging to overcome, and Judah refused to give in to the constant pull of his addiction. Besides, Hank would be furious with Judah for even considering a fall off the wagon due to his death.

Rushed footsteps tapped the sidewalk behind him and grew closer. Judah pressed his palms to his eyes, fighting back tears he wanted no one to see.

Sasha rounded the corner and ran toward him. He held up a hand to stop her until he saw the fear etched into her green eyes. "The man who attacked me was in the crowd."

He straightened and pulled his gun from his holster. "Show me."

"I would, but he's gone now. I don't know where he went. What if he's following me?"

Judah glanced back to the street but saw no one walking their way. He scanned the building and radioed the patrol officers securing the perimeter. "Any eyes on our suspect?"

The radio clicked with static then cleared. "Not sure if it's our suspect but I've got an armed man on the roof of the tavern, across the street from our crime scene. Need backup to pursue."

Judah looked up and spotted the man while three officers took off, crossed the street and entered the four-story building. The suspect raised a long-barreled rifle and aimed it toward Judah and Sasha's location. They were sitting ducks. Nowhere to hide. Unless they ran into the parking garage. He grabbed Sasha's hand and pulled her with him. "Come on."

He waited for the familiar sound of a shot fired but all was quiet except for their feet pounding against concrete.

Once inside the parking shelter, Sasha stopped and bent forward to catch her breath. "Where did the officer say he was?"

"On the roof across the street."

She moved away from the large drive-in opening and looked around. "What now?"

"We figure out an alternate route to get you out of here."

A woman sitting in a glass booth absorbed in a ratted-up paperback barely glanced up when they approached. Judah pressed his badge against the glass. "You need to get out of here. For your own safety."

The woman hopped off her stool, dropped her book and disappeared around the corner. The last thing he needed in case the gang members decided to follow them into the parking structure was an innocent bystander getting hurt or killed. Once the woman was gone, he pulled Sasha through the maze of cars and placed a call to dispatch. "I need backup in the parking garage at the corner of Main Street and Fourth."

"Units are there, across the street. We got a call about a sniper—"

"I know about the sniper but I still need a couple of units to cross the street for backup inside the parking garage."

Before he could get out more details, two men entered from a side street onto their level.

Both wore black with piercings and tattoos to spare. The taller one was Coby Evans, the NX5 leader Sasha had identified in his database.

The sniper wasn't planning to shoot them. Not with the heavy cop presence. He was a distraction so the man who'd attacked Sasha earlier could hunt her down in the garage and take her out quietly.

Judah glanced over the half wall. The parking garage was built into a steep bank and even though they'd entered from the street level at the front of the structure, the rear of the garage was at least thirty feet off the ground. Two more levels extended below and made the jump a recipe for injuries. They had no way out. He rounded a corner and pulled Sasha down between a large truck and an SUV, keeping his voice low. The two gang members hadn't seen them yet, but they were searching. "Do you have your weapon on you? We may have to shoot our way out of this one."

"Always. I just didn't want to have to shoot someone on my first week back."

"If you don't, then we might both end up dead."

Sasha retrieved her weapon, checked her magazine and

racked the first bullet into the chamber. "There's no way I'm dying in a parking garage."

Judah nodded toward the exit. "I can cover while you make a run for it. Get back to those cop cars up there and have them take you to our safe house."

"I can try."

They rose up together, using the vehicles as cover, and Sasha ran for the exit, but she didn't get far before Coby and his friend opened fire. Sasha lunged back behind the SUV next to Judah. He fired a couple of rounds to hold their attackers off, then hunkered down beside her again. "One down."

Judah fired another round of shots and missed Coby a second time. The man had gained some ground and was getting closer. He'd backed them into a corner, and there was no way out. "I'm out of ammo. Do you have an extra magazine?"

Sasha tossed him one, stood and fired three rounds. More sirens sounded and cop cars filled the entrances. Within seconds, officers fanned out through the entire structure.

Her arm lowered, and she looked back at Judah. "All clear."

"You shot him?" Judah popped up for a view.

"Not exactly. He ran."

"Where to?"

"Back through those cars somewhere. Maybe he jumped the wall."

"We'll find him." Judah walked toward the one suspect lying on the ground, kicked the weapon out of reach and checked him for a pulse. The man was still alive. Judah cuffed his hands and put pressure on his wound to control the bleeding. "Dispatch. We need an ambulance."

He looked at Sasha then nodded toward their victim. "Ever seen him before?"

She shook her head. "Only Evans."

Several officers walked toward them along with a couple of paramedics, who loaded the victim onto a stretcher. Sirens blared as they fled for the hospital.

Judah handed off the scene to one of the senior members of their team, then walked back to the front of the garage and pointed to the cameras. "You think these are active?"

Sasha stepped into the exit lane and looked up into the corner. The camera was right over her head. "Let's hope so. Maybe we can find the woman from the booth."

"Sounds like a—"

Tires squealed, and a black van barreled toward her from the opposite side of the garage. Multiple officers pulled their weapons and fired shots at the vehicle. Judah couldn't see Coby's face but he knew the man was making a run for it. Headlights brightened, and Sasha stood frozen in the exit lane, right in the path of the reckless vehicle.

Judah looked back at Sasha. If she didn't move, the van would hit her.

"Sasha."

She ignored his call, raised her arm and fired three rounds right into the windshield of the getaway vehicle.

Judah leaped and slammed into her body, knocking her to the ground. The van swerved, missing them, jumped the curb and barreled into the street.

They rolled away into a wall. Judah didn't move. Sasha remained in his arms, shaking from the close call.

"You okay?" he asked.

She nodded and sat up.

Judah grabbed his radio from his belt. "Dispatch, 372-Adam, we have a 10-78. BOLO on a black van, license plate JHP-1645. They are headed south on Fourth Street. We have two units in pursuit but need all units on this."

"Three, seven, two-Adam, dispatch. All units respond."

The officers in the garage ran for their cars in pursuit of the suspect. Judah extended a hand and helped Sasha to her feet. "I can call another ambulance."

"No, thanks. Let's go."

"But you hit your head when we landed. You need to see a doctor, or at the very least head home and rest."

"Stop babying me and let's get this guy." She moved toward the exit and headed up the hill toward his SUV. Judah followed.

"We can't let Coby get away," she said. "Not after what he did to Hank."

Judah got behind the wheel, and Sasha slid into the passenger seat. There was no convincing her to get checked out by the paramedic, and he didn't have time to argue. He took off down the same road where they'd last seen the van. Two patrol officers in pursuit radioed an update. "Code E."

"Great." Judah pressed his brakes, pulled to the side of the road and waited for traffic to clear.

Sasha shifted in her seat. "E? I'm still learning all your codes. Which one is that?"

"They lost him."

He did a U-turn and drove back to the crime scene. Gail Singer, the medical examiner, motioned for him from the entrance of Hank's building. "I've gotta go back in. Looks like the medical examiner wants to talk."

He waved a hand, and Gail disappeared inside.

"Don't worry about me." She unbuckled her seat belt. "I'll head back down to the parking garage and see if I can get us some video footage of the van to help us find him later."

"We've got officers that can do that. I think it might be better if you head home. Get some rest."

"Are you trying to get rid of me, Judah?"

Maybe he was. He focused better when she wasn't there. With her by his side, too many memories and emotions cropped up. "I'll come by your mom's house in the morning to get your statement, and then we need to get you into WITSEC."

Her body stiffened, and she pulled the door handle. "Witness protection? No need. I've got four sisters in law enforcement."

"And one of them is a US marshal. She'll tell you WITSEC is your best option to keep you safe. You can be in a new town by tomorrow night, away from these guys, who will keep coming for you until you're dead."

Sasha shook her head. "I'm not entering WITSEC—" She placed her hand on the door handle and hesitated. "—and don't come to the house. I'll be at the department in the morning for work. We can wrap up any reports then."

Judah watched her step from the car and fought the mixed emotions she always stirred up in him. He wasn't sure he could be in the same town, working every day in the same department with her.

The pain still ran deep. He'd only been sober for a year, and the memories of their past often tempted him to drink. The heartache and pain of their breakup had left deep scars and he wasn't sure he could handle revisiting those feelings every day.

He didn't blame her for his horrible choices. Those were all his own, but sometimes when the past cropped up without warning, the lure of numbing the pain outweighed his discipline. That was one risk he wasn't willing to take, but first, he had to make sure she was safe. The NX5 members that came after her today wouldn't stop until she was dead. As the only eyewitness to the murder, he'd have to keep her out of their crosshairs if he wanted Hank's killer in prison. After that, he could leave Shadow Creek for good.

Sasha left the crime scene in her late father's restored 1953 truck and drove toward the Kane family ranch. Her head throbbed, her cheek ached and she wasn't sure she could make the forty-minute drive home without a dose of coffee and a piece of apple pie from Sally's Diner. The restaurant owner was famous for her homemade desserts, and today seemed like a perfect day to kick healthy habits aside for some comfort food. She called in a to-go order.

Two pieces would do the trick and elicit several hugs from Bodie when she got home. There was nothing better than her son's toddler kisses, and after the day she'd had, he was the only one she wanted to see.

Judah still didn't know about their son. The man needed time to grieve his best friend, prepare for the burial and process her return to the precinct. Or maybe that was just her excuse to justify not telling him.

Once she dropped this bomb, both their lives would be tangled together for the foreseeable future, and she wasn't sure that was something Judah wanted. He could barely even work the crime scene with her present today. Their interactions had been awkward at best when he wasn't trying to keep her alive.

Perhaps after Hank's funeral, she'd muster up the courage to tell him the truth—not for her own or Judah's sake but for Bodie. Her son deserved to know where he got his dark waves of hair and bright blue eyes. He deserved to know his father.

Raindrops dotted her windshield and scattered neon colors across the glass as she passed underneath Sally's Diner sign. Several streetlights lit up the parking lot, and the place was packed on a Friday night. Seemed like all of Shadow Creek was there. Sasha drove around the building twice before finding a spot in the back overflow.

She stepped from her truck, breathed in the scent of fried food that not even the weather could diffuse and dashed through the entrance door as the rain turned heavy again. She shook the wetness from her jacket and noted three officers seated in a side booth. One of them looked familiar, but since she'd not really spent any time in the department yet, she wasn't sure if she should speak or not.

The blond one met her gaze and gave her a slight smile with a nod before walking over to where she stood and asking the server to fill his coffee mug. "Didn't I see you at the crime scene today at Hank Adler's office?"

"Yeah."

"You're our new photographer, right?"

"I'm a cop first, but yes, I'll be documenting all our crime scenes."

The server slid his topped-off coffee across the counter. "Did you know the victim today?" the officer said.

"He was a good friend of mine. We grew up together."

"That makes the job hard."

"One of the many downsides, I suppose." She motioned to one of the servers. "Is the order for Sasha Kane ready?"

"You're one of the Kane sisters?" The officer took a seat on a bar stool.

"In the flesh. Do you know my family?"

He extended his hand. "I guess we never met. I'm TJ.

Leila's ex-boyfriend. Your sister and I dated when you lived in Raleigh and broke up a few months ago."

She gave his hand a shake, then took the white bag from the waitress. "I believe I remember hearing something about that. Sorry things didn't work out."

"How is she? I haven't seen her around."

The man was clearly still hung up on Leila. "She's good, I guess. I've only been back for a couple of weeks, and most of that has been in job training. We haven't really had a chance to catch up."

"The precinct keeps us cops busy. Crime never sleeps, although I wish it took a day or two off sometimes."

"You and me both."

He glanced over his shoulder at his colleagues. "Well, I better get back to my group. Tell her I said hi, will ya?"

"Sure." Sasha watched him walk away. He seemed like a nice enough guy, and she made a mental note to ask Leila about him when they had a moment. Right now, all the Kane women were too busy to focus on love. Maybe things would slow down soon.

She pulled out her wallet and handed the server some cash for her bill, but the woman dismissed her payment. "Ms. Sally said that it's on the house and welcome home."

"Tell her thanks." Sasha dropped the ten-dollar bill in the tip jar, tucked the bag inside her jacket and headed for the door.

The storm still raged outside and didn't seem to be letting up anytime soon. Any other night, she would've waited in one of the vinyl booths, but she longed to be home. She pulled her jacket hood up and made a dash for the car, weaving through several vehicles before reaching the back lot, then pressing the key fob to unlock her door.

Her brake lights flashed red, outlining a dark shadow

of a man in her peripheral vision. She froze. He moved toward her from the back of her car, his gun aimed at her head. A black hoodie covered his eyes, but his voice held the same lisp as her attacker's. "You're one hard woman to wrangle."

"Wrangle? I'm not a horse."

He motioned to the door. "Get in. We're taking a drive."

If she got in the car, her chances of survival were slim. She didn't plan to be another murder statistic. If she was going to die, then she'd force his hand and make him pull the trigger right here in this parking lot, with plenty of witnesses on the other side of Sally's glass windows.

They'd see her fight and hear the shots. Bodie would know his mother went down strong, unwilling to surrender to evil wrapped in human flesh.

Her sweet boy's face flashed through her mind. All she'd wanted was to bring him home to Shadow Creek and provide the same idyllic childhood she'd had on the family farm, but since they'd arrived, their lives had taken a turn for the worse.

A loud crack of thunder boomed, rain poured and lightning streaked across the sky. She took a step toward the door as if she were being compliant, drawing the man in closer. The barrel of his gun pressed into her ribs. She pulled the door handle halfway and then, with a swift turn, Sasha knocked the gun from his hand, then landed an uppercut to his jaw. He stumbled backward and the gun fired off to the side.

Shouts from behind her met her ears.

"Police! Get on the ground. *Get on the ground.*"

The man grabbed and pulled her into a chokehold. TJ and his two colleagues ran across the gravel lot, guns drawn and ready to fire. The attacker's arm tightened around her neck as he dragged her toward the truck's back fender. She tucked her chin, fighting for every bit of oxygen she could get, and wrapped her fingers around his arm. He loosened his grip.

"They've got you surrounded," she choked out. "Let me go."

With the gun in his right hand, he fired three shots around the truck at the approaching officers. Sasha used his movement, stepped forward and donkey kicked him between the legs. He bent forward, and she landed another elbow to his jaw, then escaped from his grasp.

The man pointed his gun at her. She rounded the vehicle as a barrage of bullets pinged off the corner of her truck. TJ and his fellow officers returned shots and raced in their direction. She dropped to the ground, landing in a large puddle, but stayed low to avoid being hit in the crossfire. Her attacker fled into the thick trees bordering the back lot, and her sister's ex dispatched the other two officers in pursuit. He stopped and crouched near her.

Sasha's entire body shook, but she still didn't move. Water soaked her clothes and rocks poked into her abdomen, yet she was alive and uninjured. That's all that mattered. Bodie still had his mother.

TJ held out a hand. "He's gone. Are you okay?"

She pressed up from her belly and placed her gritty palm in his. "Freaked out, but okay."

"He ran into the woods—my colleagues are chasing him down. Did he hurt you?"

She stood and attempted to brush the wet dirt from her clothes, with little success. "I don't think so. At least he missed his shot. My throat's sore, but that could be from earlier today."

"I'm just a beat cop, so you want to tell me what's going on? I'm guessing this has to do with Hank's murder?"

"I'm the only one who can identify his killer."

"You saw his face?"

"I wish I hadn't."

TJ fingered one of the bullet holes in the truck's hood. "And they haven't put you into protective custody? Seems like the best answer, considering."

"I've been resisting."

"Why? This guy is dangerous. He's not going to stop coming for you."

She ran a finger across the bullet holes in the hood, too, hating the damage to her father's old farm truck, but at least she was alive. "I know."

TJ returned his gun to his holster. "I've got a buddy who owns a body and paint shop. I'll see if he can help you out."

"Thanks."

The other officers emerged from the tree line. "He's gone. We issued a BOLO on him but need a few more details about his description."

TJ nodded toward the diner door. "Let's head back inside, and I'll buy Sasha another coffee and some pie while we go over everything for the record."

She picked up what was left of the disintegrated paper bag and the last of her smushed food. So much for the comfort she hoped it would bring. Her surprise treat for Bodie was food for the squirrels now, if they got to it before the rain washed it away. She dumped the remnants in the outdoor bin and followed the officers inside. She knew TJ was right—NX5 would keep coming for her until she was eliminated. Sasha stopped walking and turned back to the truck.

"Forget something?" TJ followed.

She opened the passenger side door, searched the seat in the back. It had to be here. Her attacker hadn't had anything other than a gun in his hands when she first saw him. She closed the door and walked to the driver's side, searching everywhere. "Now I know why he was here."

"What did he take?"

"My camera's gone."

"With all the crime scene photos? You back them up, right?"

"Of course, but I like to keep the SD cards in case someone hacks my account."

She pulled out her phone and logged into her cloud database. Every photo from the crime scene was gone. "He got those, too."

"That's not good."

"Nope." She slammed her driver's door closed and walked toward the diner with TJ by her side. "Now the only evidence left in connection to his crime is—"

"You. You'll have to take the stand."

The weight of TJ's statement weighed heavy. Coby Evans would never stop coming for her, and if he'd go to these lengths just to get the photos, then she was in more danger now than ever.

THREE

Judah took one last look at his friend before the medical examiner zipped up the black bag. They'd had some good times together in this town, growing up, playing ball and hanging out with Sasha and her sisters. The three of them had been inseparable back in the day. Strange how life changed.

"I need the crime scene login sheet if I'm going to help you," Detective Nelson Turner, his partner, said, standing at Hank's office door.

The man was older by about ten years and worked circles around most of the younger officers. They could learn a few things from this seasoned cop, and Judah wouldn't be the detective he was today without his colleague.

He walked over, shook Nelson's hand and handed him the clipboard. "I thought you were on vacation."

"Got home yesterday and went by the precinct this afternoon. Sorry about Hank."

"Thanks. I'm glad you're back. I need you on this one."

Nelson hailed from the Charlotte police department, with fifteen years of narcotics experience, but his dream had been to be a homicide detective. When the position opened up at their precinct, his friend got the job.

"Has Quinn pulled you from the case yet?" He crossed under the tape.

"Not yet, and I plan to keep working until he does."

"I don't blame you. If it was my best friend, I'd do the same. Hank was a good man, even if he was a defense lawyer."

They stood for a moment in silence staring at the closed black vinyl bag. Judah's chest ached with grief, and he turned away as two of the medical examiner's assistants entered the room. Each took one end, placed the body on a stretcher and pushed Hank out, taking a piece of Judah with them. All the dark feelings from the loss of his mother surged through him, and he wasn't sure how he'd get through losing his best friend. Hank had been the only constant in his life other than work.

"I can't believe he's gone. We've got to find out who did this to him."

Nelson placed a hand on his shoulder. "We will, and I'm here for you. We'll make sure we do everything we can to find and put Hank's killer behind bars."

"Thanks. That means a lot."

Nelson dropped his hand and looked around the crime scene. "So Sasha Kane is our eyewitness? I guess you heard about how she was attacked, right?"

"Yeah. She was the one who found his body. Walked in on the killer after he'd already taken Hank's life and then he attacked her."

Nelson moved into Hank's office and scanned the room, taking in all the details. "That's not what I'm talking about. She was attacked again. At the diner."

Judah looked up from the evidence list. "What?"

"About fifteen minutes ago. The call came in. She was at Sally's, picked up some food, and a man attacked her in the parking lot. A couple of our patrol units were there and ran him off, but not before she got in a couple of good hits. Talk about spunky. That woman has it in spades."

Judah checked his radio. He'd turned down the volume so he could concentrate on the crime scene. He never heard the call come through. He shouldn't have let her head home alone. "I didn't realize she was making a stop or I would've followed her. Is she okay?"

"Yeah. Officers are following her back to her mom's house, and her sisters are there. They're gearing up to protect her."

"I wouldn't expect anything less from the Kane's."

Nelson inspected the spatter on the walls and desk. "I take it you've seen their claws a couple of times?"

Each sister had given him a piece of their mind after Sasha disappeared to Raleigh. Not that he didn't deserve their harsh words, but their judgment had done little to make her absence any easier. He'd confronted them, hoping they could provide some answers about why Sasha left, but to this day, he was still in the dark on the subject. "Let's just say the Kane sisters can be ferocious when protecting their own. Sasha couldn't have a better group of cops watching her back."

"They're not all cops, are they?"

"Leila's a cop. Chelsea's a US marshal, and Dani's a former cop turned private investigator. I think Holly's a forensic psychologist, but they're all in law enforcement and some of the best shooters I've ever seen. Good thing, too— the man threatening her is Coby Evans, leader of NX5."

Nelson straightened. "That's not good. Are you sure?"

Judah opened the image file he'd downloaded to his hard drive earlier from Sasha's cloud account. He clicked through a couple of images until he found the one of their suspect. "I haven't had a chance to go through them all yet, but she captured a photo of his tattoo. Recognize that?"

Nelson put on his reading glasses and leaned forward. "Looks like NX5. She needs to be in protective custody. Did she see the killer's face?"

"Yeah. From her statement and description, the assassin was Evans."

"You know that's a death sentence for her."

"Which is why we've got to find him before he gets to her. Again."

"And he'll keep trying until he succeeds. Is she sure he's the one who pulled the trigger on Hank? Coby's not usually the one to do his own dirty work."

"Not unless it was personal. I guess Coby took it hard when Hank lost one of their members' cases."

"Not just any case. It was Coby's brother who was convicted and then killed in prison." Nelson thumbed through the folders on Hank's desk. "Any idea where we can find him?"

"We thought he'd returned to his criminal compound on the edge of town, but if he attacked Sasha, I'm not sure where he is now. You can be sure of one thing, though. He's surrounded by his army of guards wherever he is."

"Sergeant Quinn sent officers to follow Sasha to her house. Are you going to go see her?"

"I have to get her statement. She told me she'd be at the precinct in the morning and she'd give it to me then, but I think I'll go by and check on her tonight, since she got attacked again. I'm sure Quinn will put a protective detail on her unless she goes into WITSEC."

Nelson shot him a look. "You sure it's a good idea for you to go to her home?"

"No, but we don't have enough detectives to work Hank's

case as it is, and if Quinn decides to boot me from the case, then I can help with protection duty and free up another officer to help you. We need as many resources we can get."

Nelson lifted a folder from Hank's desk. "I'm not sure who I should be more concerned about, you or Coby."

"Why do you say that?"

"You've got a challenging past with Sasha, plus you haven't seen her in three years and now you're going to visit her? Sounds like a recipe for disaster."

Judah looked at his watch. "This is about solving Hank's murder and keeping a vulnerable woman safe. That's all."

"And if you truly believe that, then you're further gone than I imagined."

Judah's phone buzzed. "Quinn's ears must've been burning." He flashed the screen toward Nelson, then answered his superior's call.

"Do we have Coby Evans in custody yet?" Judah asked.

"There's an ongoing search for him, but nothing yet. Where are you right now?"

"I'm at the crime scene."

Quinn's chair creaked through the line. He was probably leaning back in the old thing as he often did right before he delivered bad news. "You know you can't be investigating this case."

"Hear me out. Yes, Hank was my best friend, but he's not family, and I'm the department's expert on NX5. We have an eyewitness who places their leader, Coby Evans, at the scene. We have photos that back up her story, and Hank reported an assault by Coby a few weeks ago. I know these guys better than anyone. You have to let me work this case."

Silence emanated through the phone. "I'll let you consult, but I'm giving the case to Nelson and Leila Kane."

"Sasha's sister? She's as close to this case as I am."

"She's younger than you, Sasha and Hank, by five years and barely remembers him. You were his best friend. Out of the two of you, she's the next best choice."

"Come on, Sergeant. I can do this."

"Sorry. Not this time. However, I want you to oversee the protection detail for Sasha. Apparently, she's refusing to enter WITSEC with her son, but we need to make sure they stay safe until we get Coby off the streets."

Quinn's words sliced through him. "Did you say *son*?"

Papers ruffled through the speaker background and Judah turned to look at Hank's desk. He shuffled through the folders and found the one with Sasha's name on the tab, then flipped through the documents.

Quinn came back on the line. "Yeah. Here it is. One son. Age two. Bodie Kane."

Judah flipped past the first page, which was mostly covered in blood, and scanned the rest of the documents in the folder. The information listed matched what Quinn had told him, but one line caught his attention even more.

Father: Judah Walker

His blood ran cold. After all this time and Sasha never bothered to mention they had a son together? He leaned against the wall to steady the swirl of emotions flooding through him. That was what she'd planned to discuss with him tonight. According to the documents in his hands Hank was helping her with custody arrangements, but surely she was mistaken. Judah couldn't be a father. He could barely hold his own life together much less be the second most important person in a child's life. He was a recovering alcoholic, a decent detective, even a loyal friend but a father was something he could never be. Not now. Not ever.

* * *

By the time Sasha returned to her family's ranch, her head pounded something awful, dried mud stained her clothes and the bruises on her neck and face had darkened. The rain had cleared, though, and she cut the truck engine in the driveway, instructed the two patrol officers where to park and sat for a moment to enjoy the serenity. As soon as she entered her family's home, she'd be peppered with a thousand questions regarding the day's events.

The large white farmhouse sat on a slight hill, and interior lights cast a warm, homey glow into the yard. Fireflies danced through the thick tree line surrounding ten acres of her family's private land. She'd grown up with wonderful memories here and wanted the same kind of experience for her son. The serenity and belonging were the reasons she'd returned home.

She lifted the new bag of apple pies from the passenger seat and had just started for the door when the sweetest voice filled her ears.

"Momma. You home."

She looked up from the sidewalk path as Bodie climbed down the wraparound porch, one step at a time, and toddled as fast as his little legs would go. He threw his chubby arms around her neck while she smothered him in kisses, inciting giggles.

"What are you still doing up? It's after eight o'clock."

"Had to say night-night." He pressed his finger to her nose.

She glanced up at her mother, who waited at the top of the steps. The glow of the porch light didn't extend to Sasha's location, keeping her bruises hidden from the woman who loved her unconditionally. She hated to make her mother worry, but with a few more steps into the light, the sight of her face would trigger an interrogation.

"He's been standing by the door since I fed him his bedtime snack thirty minutes ago, wanting you to tuck him in."

Sasha lifted her son in her arms and trudged forward. Time to face the inevitable. Her mom gasped when she saw Sasha's face and clothes. "My goodness, child. What happened to you?"

"Momma got an ouchie?" Bodie's fingers touched her cheek. She pretended to bite his hand, launching her son into another round of giggles. If only her mother was as easy.

"Sasha Noelle Kane? You tell me what happened." Her mother's hand popped to her hip.

"It's a long story, and one I'd rather not tell in front of little ears."

"No wonder your sisters have been huddled in the living room whispering for the last fifteen minutes. I can't believe they didn't tell me."

Sasha hugged her mother and gave her a kiss on the cheek, then reached for the screen door. "Let me get Bodie to bed, shower and then I'll fill you in—"

"Surprise!"

She almost jumped back onto the porch with her son tightly in her grasp. Her four sisters popped out from every nook and cranny in the entire open living room. They wore party hats, and a large banner stretched across the center of the room with the words *Welcome Home* decorated in glitter. "Y'all scared me."

Bodie clapped his hands. "Me kept secret."

"Yes, you did." Sasha tweaked his nose. "I'm impressed."

Scents of fried chicken, mashed potatoes and peach cobbler wafted from the kitchen. No wonder the entire Kane troupe was there. Her mother's cooking won awards at the county fair, and she'd gone all out with the menu as well as the patio decorations.

A rectangular table held her mother's finest china, while white twinkle lights hung from the trellis, giving the space a holiday feel. The front door closed behind her.

"We decided to give you a welcome-home dinner, but at this late hour, everything is probably cold."

Chelsea, her oldest sister, dismissed the notion with a wave of her hand. "It's 8:00 p.m., Mom. Not that late."

"It is for this little guy. His bedtime was an hour ago." Sasha lowered her son to the floor. "Bodie, do you care to go play in the front room for a little while? I need to chat with your aunts and Nana for a minute. I'll come get you when I'm done and tuck you into bed."

Her little boy shuffled into the other room with his teddy bear tucked under his arm and grabbed up his truck. She turned back to the crowd of her sisters, who now noticed the bruising on her neck and face.

Chelsea gave her a hug. "Leila filled us in on what happened. We want to know every detail, and we've already been discussing a plan to protect you."

Sasha's mother shook a finger at her daughters. "You girls knew about this and didn't tell me? I wouldn't have gone to all this party trouble had I know what had happened. Why didn't you fill me in?"

"I'm sure they didn't want to worry you before they had to." Sasha moved into the open kitchen with her sisters in tow and took a seat at the bar, then gave them the condensed version of the day's events, from Hank's murder to the attacks at the law office and the restaurant.

"That's awful. I can't believe Hank's gone. You've been

friends with him and Judah for years." Holly sat on the stool beside her. "With this group, there's no way anyone will get to you or Bodie. We'll make sure of that, and if you need to talk, I'm your girl."

"I can't believe he's gone, either." Sasha took the mug of hot tea her mother handed her. "Since I've been back, he's helped me so much. He was fine this morning when I dropped all the paperwork off, but then when I went back for the meeting…"

Leila, a tough police detective and next to youngest sister, placed a hand on hers. "That must've been awful. I've been assigned to investigate the case with Detective Nelson Turner. Maybe we can go over a few questions I have later."

"I figured they'd remove Judah from the investigation. I'm sure he's pretty upset."

"He is. But Sergeant Quinn said he was too close to this one and asked me to step in."

"Understandable. I'll tell you the entire story after I put Bodie to bed."

"I want a story, too, Momma," Bodie said as he toddled around the corner and rubbed his sleepy eyes.

"Of course, my sweet. We'll read your favorite book."

Danielle, Leila's twin, gave her a side hug but kept her opinions to herself. Her youngest sister was the quiet one in the group but tougher than all of them combined. She was the observant one, which made her a great private investigator. She'd built a strong network of informants through the years—something Sasha might tap into if NX5 continued to come for her.

One thing about the Kane sisters—they could handle anything as long as they were together. And after tonight, she'd need every one of them to keep her alive.

FOUR

Judah sped through the streets of his hometown, trying to make sense of what he'd seen. If Sasha had returned with a son, then one question nagged him: Why hadn't she told him he was the father? Surely she would've told him if she'd been pregnant when she left Shadow Creek three years ago.

They'd both been different people back then—young and in love. Foolish, when he looked back now on their entire time together. He'd partied way too much, and things sometimes got out of hand. Now he realized, after getting sober, that his addiction was his way of coping with his parents' divorce and his mom's death. Sasha had provided him with the love he craved—maybe a little too much—but he'd taken her for granted.

He drove past the old haunts they used to frequent with Hank. They'd played football together in high school while Sasha cheered them on from the stands. After graduation, he and Sasha went through the police academy together while Hank did his undergrad at the local university. Judah shared an apartment with his best friend but spent most of his days with Sasha, taking classes, studying for tests or practicing their shooting at the range. She usually schooled him on the latter.

The only time they hadn't lived near each other was when his friend went to law school up north. Hank had said those were the loneliest three years of his life and he couldn't wait to return to Shadow Creek to start his own practice.

Judah pressed the back of his hand to his eyes to clear his blurred vision and rolled down the window. Cool night air helped to stem his emotions. One of his worst nightmares had come true, but he'd have time to grieve later. Right now, he had to talk to Sasha.

His headlights cast an eerie shadow when he turned into the Kane family drive and drove underneath their branded farm sign. Acres of ranchland stretched toward the large two-story house seated on a small hill. One large barn and several small outbuildings dotted the landscape, but most of the animals were put up for the night, except for one cat. Bristow sat atop a fence post and meowed when he drove by.

"Yeah. I know. I blew it."

Judah pulled up to the house, climbed the front steps and knocked on the door. He glanced at his watch. Nine p.m. He hoped Sasha wasn't asleep. Someone must still be up, since lights shone through several of the downstairs windows.

He knocked again then stepped back, swatting away gnats attracted to the outside porch light. The last thing he needed was one to end up in his eye when Sasha or one of her sisters answered the door. The latch clicked, and Holly let him inside.

"I need to talk to Sasha." He stepped into the foyer, not waiting for her to invite him inside.

"I'll go get her."

Holly disappeared down a hallway and Judah looked into the living room on his right.

A dark-headed, blue-eyed boy dressed in superhero pajamas stood, staring at him with a toy in his hand. He couldn't be more than two years old—and looked just like Judah's baby photos.

Everything around Judah and the boy seemed to fade. He took in the details of his son's face—his cute nose, the sleepiness of his eyes, the innocence in the look he was giving him right now. The rage he'd felt at Sasha for keeping this secret from him faded as the little boy's chubby hand ran across the wheels of his toy truck. This was his son. Judah was a dad. In some ways, that truth scared him to death, but more than anything, it challenged him to be a better father than the man who'd left him and his mother high and dry when they needed him the most. He'd never leave his son.

The toddler held out an object. "Car."

Judah stepped into the room and scanned the makeshift play area.

Several books were stacked on the couch, with one open to a photo of a bulldozer digging in dirt. A variety of toys littered the rug and a small whiteboard sat on an easel, with a little boy holding the hand of a dark-haired woman.

One day he could only hope to be included in his son's artwork. Sasha had clearly helped draw the picture—and had clearly left Judah out of the drawing.

The little boy blew air from his lips, causing them to vibrate into an engine noise, then tilted his head as he pushed the truck around the track. Judah's mother had kept a Christmas photo of him in the exact same pose attached to the refrigerator for years. In fact, he still had the photo somewhere in a box with other mementos from his childhood. He'd have to go through the items and see if there were any toys his mother saved that he could share with Bodie.

If Sasha had known she was pregnant when she left, then he understood her reason for keeping her secret back then. He'd had too many issues to be a father then, but he was different now. He was sober, had been promoted to a detective and had a strong network of friends to keep him in check. And he'd always believed there was more for him.

Unanswered questions made sense for the first time in years. Sasha had left town to have a baby. His baby. Lamplight cast an angelic glow on the child's face—Judah's face, only younger, softer and with a sweet smile that belonged to the woman who rounded the corner of the room. Sasha stopped when she saw him.

He locked eyes with her, his head spinning with a million questions, but one rushed to the tip of his tongue.

"Why didn't you tell me?"

Memories of the night they spent together flashed through his mind, and the result of their decision wrapped his small arms around his mother's neck when she lifted him from the floor.

Sasha crossed the room. "I was planning to tell you today at our meeting, but then…" She squared her shoulders and swallowed. "Well, you know. I thought with Hank's death it might be too much."

He couldn't take his eyes off the child in her arms. He'd missed so much of his life already. His first smile and laugh. His first steps and words. All because Sasha left and made a choice to keep him in the dark, until now.

She stepped toward him. "This is your son, Bodie."

Judah held out his palm for a low five, and the little boy touched his hand—so gentle and small, barely reaching the bottom of his fingers, but it pierced him straight to his soul.

It was official.

His life would never be the same from this point forward. He called them sticky moments—memories that never left your mind. The bad ones haunted him, and he had plenty of those, but the good ones were few and far between. In fact, this one was the best of all—but also overwhelming.

"Excuse me." He backed away. "I need a minute."

He exited the home and leaned against the front door when it closed behind him. His heart raced, and he inhaled to try and catch his breath. Even pacing back and forth across the creaky porch did little to alleviate the panic.

Who was he kidding? He couldn't be a father. His old man had taken off when he was sixteen, and his mom had died twelve years later. He'd never wanted a drink more than right now, but he refused to give in to the addiction that had started with simply wanting to fit in with some older kids at school. After his dad left, he drank more, blaming his father for every drop. Then his mom passed, and he blamed God. Alcohol numbed his pain, and the idea that Sasha had cut him from his son's life for two years was the most painful moment in his life to date.

A rush of anger rose to the surface at the inadequacy of his past, the woman who betrayed him and a God who took his parents from him. How could one man endure so much and survive without some kind of vice?

A breeze blew and rustled the large oak tree where Sasha's swing still hung to this day. He wondered if Bodie had played on it yet. He'd have to make sure it was secure so his son wouldn't get hurt. He inhaled the fresh mountain air, calmed his mind and determined to set a better example for Bodie than his father had for him.

How dare Sasha keep his son away all this time. They'd

been apart for three years and she couldn't even pick up the phone. He would've moved to Raleigh and helped her with the baby if she'd only let him be a part of his son's life. He'd tried to visit after she'd been gone a couple of months, but when he arrived, she'd refused to see him and her aunt shooed him away. Now he knew why.

He leaned against the railing and looked out over the acres of pastureland. She'd loved him at one time. At least that's what she'd said, but was this how a person acted when they were in love?

Maybe they had gone too far, and marriage wasn't something he'd wanted back then, but they could've worked something out. He might've changed his mind if he'd only known about the baby, but the way she left only proved one thing—she'd never really loved him at all.

If she did, then she would've told him. She would've stayed. God knows he wasn't living right back then, but he'd done anything for her. Then again, she'd asked him to stop drinking but he didn't listen. He'd clearly loved alcohol more than her and she didn't want her son to have a drunk dad. How could he blame her for that?

The door clicked behind him, but he didn't turn around. He couldn't face her. Not yet.

"What do you want to know?" Sasha's voice was quiet, timid.

"How old is he?"

"Just turned two."

Two years of his son's life gone. Those were moments he'd never get back. Heat rose into his face again, and he turned, ready to yell, but a small hand smacked the living room window before he could say a word. Bodie peeked out from behind a curtain and stared up at him. Those innocent eyes and that lopsided grin stole his heart before one of her sisters snatched the boy up.

The last thing he wanted was for Bodie to witness an angry conversation with his mother. He pulled his keys from his pocket. "Ride with me?"

"Sure. Let me grab my bag."

She stepped back inside for a moment, then returned and climbed into the passenger seat of his brand-new truck. He inhaled the leather scent and backed out of the driveway, not sure how to turn his words into a productive conversation. He had so much to lose if he didn't handle this well.

The tension inside him built with every passing mile. He gripped the wheel until his knuckles turned white and his jaw ached from clenching his teeth. He couldn't take the silence any longer and pulled into one of their former hangouts—the pier at Shadow Creek.

A gravel lot on the left bordered the water and offered a path down to an old wooden dock. Rocks crunched under the tires as he parked, then he exited the vehicle.

He didn't open the passenger door for her like he used to do when they dated. Instead, she slammed it and followed him onto the long, narrow boardwalk that led to the water. Her flip-flops clicked against her heels, but she didn't say a word.

He stopped when he reached the end and stared at the rushing current below. Recent rains had raised the level quite high and it looked more like a river than a creek. White foam swirled around boulders, highlighted by a full moon streaking across the chaotic rapids.

Sasha's arm brushed his as she stood beside him, quiet. Her long, slender fingers gripped the rail.

"Is Bodie the reason you left?" he asked.

"More like the reason I didn't come back sooner. I didn't find out I was pregnant until later."

"Then you left because of me."

"I left because of us. Our relationship wasn't going well, and I didn't know how to fix it anymore. I needed a fresh start to help me get things in perspective. I planned on coming back after a few weeks, but then I found out I was pregnant with Bodie and my entire life changed."

"I understand the feeling." He pushed back from the railing to face her. "And you're sure he's—"

"Yes, I'm sure." Her knuckles turned whiter. "I haven't been with anyone but you, if you must know. How can you even ask that question? You've seen him. He looks just like you."

"A lot of men have blue eyes."

"He's yours, Judah."

Her quick response brought him a bit of relief and anxiety all at the same time.

"You could've called and told me."

"Every time I picked up the phone, I remembered our last night together. I'd never seen you like that."

One of the darkest times in his life had culminated in the worst argument they'd ever had. He'd shown up at her house drunk a few days after burying his mother. "Not my best moment."

"When your mom passed, I thought you'd wake up, but instead you got worse. I lost you with her, and even though I tried everything, I knew I couldn't get you back. Your addictions were too strong. So, I left. I didn't find out I was pregnant until I'd been in Raleigh for almost a month."

Judah leaned against the rail and folded his arms across his chest. "I went to rehab, tried to call you and even wrote you letters, but you never responded. When I got out, I even came to see you, but you refused me. Don't you think I had a right to know about my son?"

"Not when your drinking could put Bodie in danger. I heard things got worse before they got better. I couldn't risk exposing him to that kind of lifestyle."

He was surprised she'd been keeping tabs on him. "Another story from your sisters?"

"Don't blame them. They were very protective once they found out about Bodie."

"Believe me. I've seen the Kane sisters in action but they still could've told me. I never hurt you when we were together. Not physically. All this time and none of them ever said a word to me. I even worked with Leila at the precinct."

"They're my family, Judah."

He faced her. "And Bodie is *my family*."

"I had to protect him."

He couldn't fault her for her reasons. His alcohol addiction had gained control over his behavior for a time, but that was in the past. If she'd been the one with the problem, he would've stuck around and gotten her the help she needed instead of abandoning her. "Did they also tell you I went to rehab and cleaned up my life?"

"They did."

"Then if I'm such a bad influence, why are you back?"

Sasha climbed onto the top rail and sat with her back to the water, a breeze blowing her dark hair from her face. Moonlight reflected in her eyes and he looked away, not willing to soften his stance because of her beauty. Her life choices hadn't been the best when they dated, either. She'd partied right alongside him most of the time.

"My aunt was getting older, and Bodie's energy level wore her out. Plus, I missed my mom and my sisters. When

Leila called about the forensic photographer job at the precinct, I decided to come home."

"*You* decided." Movement caught Judah's eye, and he looked past her to the parking area, where a raccoon dug in the trash can for a late-night snack. He looked back to her. "I want to know my son, Sasha. I deserve to spend time with him and be a part of his life."

"I agree. I want you to know him, too, especially since you've been sober for a year. That's why I reached out to Hank and drew up a custody agreement. That's what we were supposed to discuss today."

Heat rushed through him again. "You told my best friend, planned out a future for me that I had no say so in. Don't you think I should've been a part of that?"

He didn't know whether to be more angry at her or Hank for keeping such a life-altering secret.

"And that discussion was supposed to start tonight, with Hank there to help us. He's the one who encouraged me to have the meeting with you. He was helping me, Judah. He was helping us."

Her hand touched his arm, but he pulled away. He needed time to process everything she told him. The entire town of Shadow Creek had known about his son, it seemed. Everyone except him. He felt like an idiot.

"There's just some things you don't keep from your best friends, Sasha, and this is one of them."

"Hank was only try—"

Gunfire popped and whizzed past Judah's head. He lunged for Sasha, hitting her full force. The weakened railing gave way. Cold mountain water enveloped his body and he fumbled for her fingers, but the swift current pulled them apart. Underwater boulders slammed into him, and his lungs burned for oxygen. He kicked and broke through to the surface. Frantic, Judah scanned the water. Sasha was nowhere in sight, but a large tree had fallen into the water a few yards in front of him. The current was headed straight for the branches. He swam to his right, but the strong rapids propelled him into the watery trap.

Swift water swept Sasha downstream. She'd grown up kayaking on this river and used her skills to position her feet in front of her, then pulled through the current with her arms and bobbed her head to the surface. "Judah?"

No response.

She shouted louder, but hearing anyone over the roar of the rapids would be a challenge, much less spotting anyone in the darkness. The full moon cast a bit of a glow until the cloud cover obscured the light.

Her hands and arms tingled with cold and her feet were already numb. Despite the summer temperatures being in the eighties during the day, the cold runoff from the mountains kept the water icy. If she didn't get out soon, hypothermia would overtake her.

Sasha mustered up a bit of energy, determined to see her kid again, and fought her way to a calmer eddy. Her muscle coordination was already inhibited, but she didn't give up and crawled onto a pebbled shore, rocks and sticks digging into her knees. She pushed to her feet and scanned the water again. Judah was a strong swimmer but this creek, when the levels were high, had claimed multiple lives over the years, many of whom she'd never dreamed would drown. She prayed he wouldn't become another statistic.

The clouds shifted, and the full moon lit up the night sky. Movement, about fifty feet up, grabbed her attention. Judah flailed an arm, his body trapped against a tree collapsed in the river. The force of water pressed against him, and with each attempt to escape, he slipped farther under the surface. If he was as cold as she was, then it wouldn't be long before the river claimed his life.

Sasha rushed up the bank, slipping on loose rocks and debris, but made the trek to solid ground. She ran to his position and extended a long, broken branch. "Grab hold. I'll pull you out."

He looked exhausted. If he wanted her help, then he had to let go of his only lifeline. If she missed, then she might not see him again.

"Make a big jump for the branch." She pushed her wet hair from her eyes.

He nodded, released his grip and lunged for the lifeline. Water swept over him, and he disappeared underneath the surface. "Judah!"

Several seconds passed. No weight pulled on the other end of her branch, and she didn't see him. She pressed the limb farther into the water. The natural sieve of the fallen tree must have him trapped. If Judah didn't grab hold soon, Bodie might never know his father. Her arms grew heavy with the weight of the waterlogged branch, and she stepped farther into the current the familiar sting of tears burning her eyes. *Please, God. Don't let him die.*

Downward pressure jerked the end of the branch, and she stumbled forward but caught her balance on a large rock. Judah's hand broke through the surface of the water, and she used her legs to pull. One step back after another until his head broke the surface.

He floated forward and crawled onto the beach, collapsing on his back beside her. His blue T-shirt adhered to his toned chest muscles and lifted with every heavy breath. "Thanks."

She followed his gaze to the stars dotting the black sky. "I thought you were a goner."

"That makes two of us." Judah sat up and coughed, his body shivering from his cold, wet clothes.

"We need to get warm." Sasha stood and held out a hand. The warmth of the summer night helped, but without the sun to heat them back up, hypothermia could take hold. "I'm sure your brand-new truck has a good heater."

"Let's just hope the shooter's gone." He grasped her hands and rose to his feet. "They're coming after you because you saw Hank's killer."

She released his hand. "I know."

"Not just any killer, but Coby Evans, leader of NX5."

"That's not good."

He walked toward the parking lot path. "I'll call Sergeant Quinn and get a US marshal to admit you and Bodie into Witness Protection. They can move you far away and offer 24-7 protection. Coby and his gang are dangerous here, but once you're out of his vicinity, maybe he'll drop his vendetta."

"Don't they have connections across the country?"

"Mostly in the Southeast, so we can move you west and find a place where you'll be safe."

Sasha slowed her steps at his suggestion. "But I'll have to leave my family again. I just got home. And what about you?"

"What about me?"

"Don't you want to spend time with your son?"

He stopped walking and faced her. "Of course I do, but this man isn't going to stop until you're dead. He tried to assassinate you twice today, and he won't hesitate to take you both out, along with anyone else who gets in his way."

His theory made sense, but living a lie in a new town

wasn't the way she wanted to raise her son. "I've got Chelsea. She's a US marshal and can protect us here."

"I don't think the program really works like that. The way they protect you is by relocating you and Bodie, breaking all ties with family and loved ones. US marshal policies won't allow Chelsea to keep you in your hometown, and since you're her sister, I doubt she'd be allowed to protect you or Bodie anyway."

"If we break all ties, that includes you."

Judah ran a hand through his wet hair and twisted the bottom of his shirt to wring out the water. Sasha averted her gaze and pushed the memory of their night together from her mind. She was thankful for the darkness and the shadows hiding the flush of her cheeks.

He released the wrinkled fabric and returned to the path without any response to her obvious statement.

If she did what he asked, Bodie would never know his father. Maybe that's what Judah wanted. He'd only found out about Bodie less than an hour ago, and she'd had several months to process the idea of becoming a mother before Bodie arrived. She'd disrupted the man's world with her news, and now he wanted her to disappear again.

She stared at the back of his head as they walked, frustrated that he was ignoring her question. "Don't you want to get to know Bodie?"

"He's not used to having me in his life yet, and if you enter the program now, he won't miss me."

His words broke her heart. It was her fault Bodie was not used to having Judah in his life. She'd never given him a chance to do the right thing. God knows having a baby had changed her life forever, and she was thankful for her newfound faith, but Judah had never had that opportunity. She couldn't blame him for wanting his life to go back to normal. Maybe he'd moved on with someone else and loved another. She hadn't even thought to ask him if he had a new girlfriend. He hadn't mentioned or even hinted at a current relationship, but why should he? They were no longer together, and the man had a right to happiness.

When they reached the edge of the tree line, Judah held up a hand and scanned the parking lot. She remained behind a tree for safety.

"All clear. Looks like whoever shot at us is gone."

"As long as they don't come back."

"Another reason for you to enter WITSEC. Coby Evans is not the kind of man who'll give up if you stay in Shadow Creek. You're the only link to his crime, and if he wants you dead, he won't stop coming for you."

"You really think they can keep us safe from him?"

"Of course. That's what marshals are trained to do. They have an extremely high success rate. That's the best option for you and Bodie."

"You're sure quick to send us away. Is there something you're not telling me? Someone else I don't know about?" The idea of leaving her mom and sisters again was almost too much to bear, especially if he wanted them gone so he could be with a new love.

He stopped at the driver's side door, and his gaze narrowed. "There's no one else. My first concern is your safety. If NX5 harms you or Bodie, then my chance to get to know my son will be gone forever. I'm not letting anyone take that away from me again."

His statement stung, but he made a fair point. NX5 was known to eliminate anyone that posed a threat to their daily business, and if Judah wanted a future opportunity to know Bodie, then he'd need their son to be alive. However, WITSEC was not something a person entered without dire consequences, and giving up her family again was not something she wanted to do. Maybe Judah's intentions were good, but it felt like he wanted them gone.

Sasha shook her hair, sending drops of water down her back. "I can't leave. Not right now. If you don't want to protect us, then my sisters will."

The pained look on his face did more to chill her than her wet clothes. "It's not that." He paused for a moment, as if thinking through his next statement carefully. "I'm not afraid of being a father, Sasha. I'm afraid of losing my only son without ever getting to know him. Witness Protection would be temporary until we can find Coby Evans and put him away. Then I can get to know Bodie without the fear of someone shooting at us from the woods."

She noted he didn't mention her in the equation.

He stepped closer. "These guys are killers. Not the kind that only put a bullet through *your* skull. They're the kind that come for your entire family and everyone you love. They're known for torture, assault and murder. If you stay here, I'm scared you and Bodie will find out how evil this gang truly is. I'm not confident I can keep y'all alive if you stay."

His serious tone and intense gaze convinced her to at least consider the option. He stood close, hands on his hips and mouth within inches of hers. She fought the urge to kiss him after all these years. That door had already been closed, and she didn't need to open it right now, if ever. Sasha stepped back and rounded the truck to put some distance between them, refusing to give in to past emotions. "Looks like the shooter's gone."

"Not without leaving us a present." Judah bent forward and picked up a shell casing. "I'll turn this in as evidence and see if we can get a print or something. Although I'm sure it was one of Coby's members."

A breeze blew across her wet clothes. "I'm freezing. Let's go back to the farm. We can talk there." She reached for the door handle. "How do you think he found us? It's not like this place is teeming with people."

"He must've followed us. Or saw us leave the farmhouse."

A bolt of fear struck her. "If he was watching the farmhouse, then—"

His gaze met hers. "Bodie."

Sasha hopped into the passenger seat, buckled up and clung to the handle as Judah whipped onto the road. If anything happened to Bodie, she'd never forgive herself. Her son was everything to her, and she had to get to him before anyone else did.

If her attacker was desperate enough to shoot at her in the middle of the woods, then he wouldn't hesitate to use her son as leverage, or worse—and the man had a head start.

FIVE

Sasha burst through the front door, checked the sitting room where her son liked to play with his toys and raced through to the farmhouse kitchen. "Where's Bodie?"

Her mother stood up from the dinner table and confusion swept across her sisters' faces. "I put him to bed. He fell asleep when we were reading a book. We were waiting for you, but he couldn't keep his little eyes open, so I put him in his room. I hope that's—"

Sasha didn't wait for her mother to finish but climbed the back staircase two steps at a time. She had to get to him and make sure he was safe.

"Sasha? What's going on?" Her mother's words faded behind her as she headed down the hall to the third door on the left.

She kept moving without giving any answers. Explanations were for later—right now she had to see with her own eyes that her little boy was safe and sound in his bed.

With a turn of his door handle, she entered. The nightlight cast a dim glow around the room. Trucks and tractors dotted the wallpaper, but when she moved toward the toddler bed and pulled back the blankets, Bodie was gone.

She tossed the blankets to the floor along with the pillow. He had to be here somewhere. Maybe he'd heard her coming down the hallway and decided to play hide-and-seek. He loved the game, and his favorite hiding place was in the closet.

A rush of adrenaline tightened her chest and squeezed the oxygen from her lungs. Sasha flung open the slatted doors and flung every shoe, bag and child's game to the middle of the room. The space was empty.

"Bodie?"

Her hands shook when there was nothing left to toss. She crumpled on the floor and clutched his blanket to her face, breathing in her son's fresh baby scent. He was gone. NX5 had taken him.

The door thudded against the wall, but she didn't care who entered. Even if the men who wanted her dead came for her now, they could kill her. Death would be a welcome alternative to a life without her son.

Judah crossed the room to the toddler bed and radioed in an Amber alert, then knelt on the floor beside her. "We'll find him. I promise."

Sasha clung to his hand as if he were the only thing holding her from descending into the darkest pit of despair. "They took him. NX5 has my baby."

"He's not here?" Her mother's voice echoed from the hallway. "I put him to bed thirty minutes ago. He has to be here."

A cool breeze brushed against Sasha's arm. She looked up. Moonlight backlit the curtain as the fabric shifted. She crawled over and looked onto the roof covering the porch. A white trellis extended to the ground from the side. "This is how they took him without anyone seeing. We don't have any cameras on this side of the house."

"I'm the one who cracked a window. It was stuffy in here, and I didn't want to run the air." Her mother crossed the room and pushed the pane closed. "What about the other rooms? Have you checked those?"

Sasha pushed to her feet. "We *have* started potty training him, but he's never gone on his own at night, so he wears a diaper."

"I'll check." Judah disappeared from the room then returned. "He's not in the other rooms on this floor. I think you're right, Sasha. NX5 has taken him."

She leaned into her mother's open arms. "What are we gonna do?"

"I'm so sorry. This is my fault. I should've waited for you to get back. He wanted you to tuck him in tonight."

"That wouldn't have stopped them. You did what any good grandmother would do." Sasha took a seat in the soft rocker and fought back the nausea churning her insides. The room spun, and she lowered her head between her knees. "I'm gonna be sick."

She rushed into the bathroom across the hall and splashed cold water on her face and neck. Her body calmed, but her mind raced. If they were going to find Bodie alive, then the next forty-eight hours were important. She had to keep her wits about her.

When she emerged, Judah was standing in the hall, tucking his phone back into his pocket. "You okay?"

"No. What do we need to do to find him? I want my son back."

"I just hung up with dispatch. Officers will be here in five. We'll start a search, since they couldn't have taken him far. I'm headed outside right now to check the perimeter. Do you want to join me?"

"You go. I want to talk to my sisters. Dani's specialty is finding missing persons. I want her to oversee an individual investigation."

"Finding him won't be easy." Judah shook his head. "I don't even want to tell you this, but it's best to prepare yourself."

"What?"

"NX5 has a network of resources for human trafficking."

"I figured they'd use him to draw me out, not to sell him off to the highest bidder."

"And they may. That would actually be a better scenario for us to handle. Before we send out the masses, let me check the area around the house just to make sure the little guy didn't wander outside for a toy or something."

"Go ahead, but I'm not waiting. Time is the only advantage we have."

Judah headed back down the stairs, and Sasha heard the kitchen's screen door slam upon his exit. She looked out the window and saw him climb into his car, then out again. He moved to the side, out of sight.

"Who would do such a horrible thing?" Her mother returned the little comforter back to his bed. Tears streamed down her cheeks.

"Some very bad men." Sasha gave her mother another hug and wiped away her own tears. "For us to find him, we have to be smart, and emotions only cloud our thinking. I'm going to talk to Dani. She's got a large network of informants. Maybe she can tap them and get some information."

Sasha descended the stairs to where her sisters all stood in the living room, whispering among themselves. She took in a deep breath. "Bodie's missing, and we believe NX5 members took him."

"What can we do?" Holly asked.

"They'll do anything to keep me quiet. This is dangerous, so if you can't help, I understand. Bow out now." None of the Kane women moved a muscle.

"Good. Then let's get to work. Holly, I need you to research and find everything out you can about NX5's trafficking trade. I want to know about their real estate holdings, shipping containers, van lines and anything else that they will need to send my son God knows where. Dani, I need you to hit up all your connections and see if any—"

The screen door creaked open, and Sasha turned. Judah entered holding Bodie in his arms. Their son clung to his father, his shoulders hiccuping with soft, whimpered sobs. She rushed to Judah and pulled her son from his arms.

"Oh dear Jesus, thank you. Where did you find him?" Emotions surfaced, and she no longer held back her tears, smothering the child with wet nuzzles.

"In his booster in the back seat of your car."

Her sisters gathered around, and she shifted Bodie to her shoulder. "My car? Why would they leave him there?"

"Maybe they got spooked."

"Or wanted to spook you," her mother said.

"Well, it worked." Sasha rubbed a hand across her toddler's back and whispered soothing words into his ear. She breathed in his honey-scented baby shampoo and swiped away tears with her fingers, thankful her son was most likely too young to ever remember the frightening night. Bodie relaxed against her shoulder and fell back to sleep. "He's exhausted."

Judah placed a hand on his head. "They might've taken him as a warning."

"A warning?" She sat on one of the wooden stools in the open kitchen and shifted Bodie to her lap, rocking him back and forth.

Judah stood across from her. "They want you to know they can get to him."

"Then why leave him in the car? Why not take him and trade him for me?"

"A missing toddler will bring too much attention to their operation. News outlets, search parties and multiple teams of federal and local agents are the last thing a gang wants in their territory. They want you to stay quiet until they figure out a way to eliminate you. By moving Bodie, they're hoping to scare you into silence."

His analysis roiled inside her gut, and she knew she had to make a decision for Bodie's safety. If anything happened to him, she'd never forgive herself. "Then we'll enter WITSEC. On one condition."

"That's wise. What's the condition?" he asked.

"That you go with us."

Judah shook his head a little too quickly. "I can't. I have to find Hank's killer."

"Hank's dead, but our son is alive and well. He needs you."

He swiped a hand through his hair, now dry after their swim. She knew without him saying a word that he would never leave everything behind. All of his past, his addictions and his bad choices kept him chained to this town, and if he was unwilling to go with them after what had happened tonight, then he never would. Judah Walker left her no other choice.

Sasha stood. "Chelsea?" Her US marshal sister protected dozens of witnesses, most of them criminal snitches who were willing to roll on their gang leaders. "We're going to need your help. I'm no longer willing to take any chances and you can make sure we stay safe."

"No worries, sis. I'll get you into WITSEC."

"Instead of entering us into the program, I want to stay here. Can you keep me and Bodie safe?"

"Protocol states we must relocate you to a new place, breaking all ties to your family—"

"I'm not leaving." Sasha locked eyes with Judah as she said the words. "I need you to protect us here."

"I can, but I don't think that's your best option."

Judah placed a hand on her arm. "She's right. Staying here with Bodie is risky. Why not enter the program just until we figure out a way to dismantle NX5?"

She raised her chin. "And if I go, what's stopping them from taking out my sisters or my mother? I'm not going to run." The idea of her family being threatened or killed because of her was not an option. "My absence won't guarantee their safety, and when the Kane sisters work together we have a better chance of survival."

Chelsea pulled out her phone and began texting. "Mom, do we still have that place in the woods?"

"Of course. The Whitmore property."

"Great. I'll take some time off, clear everything with my superiors and help keep y'all safe."

Leila stepped forward and focused on Judah. "I guess you know I'll be working the homicide investigation with Nelson."

"Yeah, Sergeant Quinn called me earlier with the news. He put me on protection duty."

"Don't worry. I'll still need your help. He said you could consult, and I'm going to take full advantage of your NX5 brain."

Dani stepped from the corner. "What's the plan to keep Sasha and Bodie safe since she's refusing to go into WITSEC?"

"The plan is for Chelsea to protect us *right here*."

Leila looked back at Judah. "You think that's best?"

"Not my decision."

Sasha noted his tense jaw and wasn't sure if his frustration was from being removed from Hank's case or having to babysit her in an isolated mountain cabin for the foreseeable future.

"Don't worry, Judah," Dani said. "It won't take long for Leila to find and arrest Coby. He likes to spend his evenings at Shadow Creek Tavern."

Leila's phone vibrated, and she scrolled through the message. "Looks like Nelson's already made an arrest in Hank's murder—and it's not Coby Evans."

"That can't be right. He's the man who attacked me in Hank's office." Sasha shifted in her seat. "Who else would want Hank dead?"

"Apparently, the man who owns the coffee shop." Her sister swiped her screen as she read more details about the arrest.

"Mr. Bell? He's no killer." Judah paced the floor.

"Says here they found the murder weapon stashed in his shop, and a customer witnessed him and Hank having an argument the week before Hank was killed."

Leila held up the man's booking photo for Sasha to view. "Is this the man who was in the room with you?"

"Not even close." She took the phone from her sister's hand for a closer look. "This man is bald with a beer gut. My guy was tall, in shape, fought like an MME fighter and had dark hair. He had a scar on his left cheek and an NX5 tattoo. He matched the photo of Coby Evans in the database. I don't think Mr. Bell has any tattoos. None that we can see, anyway."

"The judge set Mr. Bell's arraignment for tomorrow."

Sasha handed the phone back to her sister. "They're going to put away an innocent man if I don't speak up."

"The investigators have your initial statement."

"Then they didn't read it. I have to tell the district attorney." She held out her hand to Judah. "Can you find his number and let me call him?"

He scrolled through his contacts, tapped the DA's number and gave the phone to Sasha.

"He's not answering." She ended the call without leaving a message, handed Bodie to her mom, then grabbed her keys and bag.

Judah stepped in front of her. "Where are you going?"

"Doesn't DA Strut live in Rockford Estates?"

"You can't go to his house. It's after eleven."

Sasha glanced at her watch. In all the chaos, she hadn't realized how late the hour was. "But Mr. Bell didn't kill Hank."

"Did you see Coby pull the trigger?" Judah asked.

"No, but he was there."

"Doesn't mean he killed Hank. Someone could've been there before Evans and shot him. Like Mr. Bell. Hank was his landlord, and I know the man was behind on his rent. They could have had an altercation that turned violent."

"I suppose." Sasha placed her bag on the kitchen table and took a seat. "Wait. That's why it took him so long to leave the scene of the crime."

"What do you mean?" he asked.

"The van almost barreled over us when he left, but that was well after Coby attacked me. I thought it was weird he didn't leave the parking garage until later. Maybe he sent some of his members back and planted the gun in Mr. Bell's shop. That would explain the delayed exit, when they almost ran us over in the garage. Don't most killers get as far as they can from the crime scene afterward?"

Leila took back her phone. "You got any proof?"

"There was a six-digit number written on Hank's hand. At first, I didn't think too much about it, because the code changes on the first of every month."

"Code? What code?" Leila asked.

"To the back service entrance of the building. Since our meeting was after hours, he gave me the number to come in that door instead of the front. That's how they got in."

"Why would it be on Hank's hand?" Dani moved from the corner of the room and took a seat at the table.

"Sometimes Hank would write things on his palm if he didn't have any paper."

Leila typed a few notes into her phone. "If Hank gave that number to you, he could've given it to any one of his clients—"

"The code automatically changed at the end of every week. Probably didn't want to forget it until he gave it to Mr. Bell," Sasha said.

"So the only people who would have the code would be the clients Hank gave the numbers to today." Judah looked at Leila. "That narrows down the number of suspects. I went through some of his digital files while waiting at the crime scene earlier, and he had a lot of enemies, but if they weren't on the schedule for today—"

"Then they wouldn't have the code. But he could've let them inside if they showed up unannounced. I'll check and see if the video footage from the lobby matches any of his current clients." Leila left the room with the phone to her ear.

Sasha turned to Judah. "I'd still like to talk with DA Strut. Maybe this new information will keep him from completely ruling out Coby. I still think he's the trigger-man, but I know we have to look at all the evidence."

"We aren't going to look at anything. That's Leila and Nelson's job. Our number one goal is figuring out how to keep you and Bodie safe, and going to talk with DA Strut is too dangerous."

"And if I don't, then Bodie and I will never be safe. I'll always be a threat to the leader of NX5." Sasha paced the floor. "Someone has to stop them, and I'm the only one who can. I have to go, Judah. You understand, right?"

"Let me figure out a way we can get you in there without a ton of eyes on you."

"You've got until 7:00 a.m. or I'm going with or without you." Sasha took Bodie from her mother's arms and headed upstairs to her bedroom.

The calm blue walls and furnishings held the scent of the fresh gardenias her mother had placed in a vase on the dresser. The flowers were from the family garden, and her mother changed them every few days as part of her hospitality routine. The woman always wanted her home ready for unexpected company, and she had plenty of guests to-night.

A cool breeze blew through the window, and after placing Bodie on the freshly washed sheets, then pushing the bed against the wall to keep him from rolling off, she pulled down the sash. No more surprises tonight.

The gentle rise and fall of Bodie's chest triggered tears in her eyes. She hated that evil had tainted her baby's world. She'd never survive if someone hurt him. The only way to keep him safe was to collect the evidence and put Coby Evans behind bars for the rest of his life.

A car door slammed outside, and Sasha moved to the window, then pulled back the curtain. Judah sat in his truck and reclined the seat back a little, then placed his phone to his ear. With all her sisters staying the night, his presence wasn't required, but he didn't leave.

When they'd thought Bodie had been kidnapped, it had shaken Judah. She'd never seen fear on his face like that before. Maybe he was different now, but she wanted more than different. She wanted a man who was surrendered to Jesus, and he wasn't there yet.

Another patrol car pulled into the driveway, and she watched Judah motioned them to guard the back side of the house. The rear of the property bordered national game lands and offered an amount of privacy few landowners possessed. Although now the isolation didn't provide more security but made the area even harder to patrol. He stepped from his car and scanned the perimeter with night-vision goggles, then climbed back inside.

In some ways, he was still the same guy she'd always known, even if he was a little more scarred from family trauma, but he'd taken steps to mature and overcome those obstacles in his life. She couldn't deny that he was still as handsome as ever, with a toned physique and blue eyes that cut through to her soul.

Would he ever forgive her for not telling him about their son sooner? If someone had kept a secret like that from her, she wasn't sure how she'd respond. Maybe they could move forward as friends and learn to coparent. That was really all she could hope for at this point.

Judah looked up and found her staring. Her heart quivered, and she released the curtain to flutter back in place, then stepped away, praying he hadn't seen her.

How she wanted him to be a part of Bodie's life, but choosing their son was his decision—one he had to make on his own. If he didn't want to be a father, then she'd figure out another way to provide Bodie with a male role model in his life. Maybe WITSEC wasn't such a bad idea. At least that way she could start fresh if Judah decided he wanted no part of their lives.

Exhaustion stung her eyes, and her body ached from her beatings. She longed for a peaceful rest, but with NX5 still lingering out there somewhere, a full night's sleep was bound to be elusive. Sasha washed up, changed clothes and crawled into bed next to Bodie, then placed a light kiss on his forehead. All the stress and worry faded from her body within seconds, and she closed her eyes.

At least for tonight, they were safe.

Judah turned his car radio to a country station, determined to come up with a plan to keep his son safe. He'd have to find another way with Sasha refusing to enter WITSEC. He couldn't blame her after being away from her family for three years, but Witness Protection was the best defense against a murderous gang like NX5.

Chelsea had mentioned the Whitmore property. He'd lived here all his life and wasn't even sure where that was located. He dialed Sergeant Quinn before considering the time.

"Sorry to bother you so late, but I wanted to give you an update. I'm stationed outside the Kane family farmhouse for the night. I'm calling about a location they mentioned. Have you ever heard of the Whitmore property?"

His superior's voice sounded groggy on the other end of the line, which wasn't a surprise since his clock read midnight. The man didn't complain or even comment on the late hour. Cops were used to getting calls at all hours of the night. "Can't say I have, but I can do a search and see what I find. How are you doing? All this trauma must be a challenge."

Judah hadn't fully processed the news about having a son and wasn't ready to share the details of such a life-altering announcement. He kept the topic focused on Hank. "I'd be better if you let me work the case instead of putting me on guard duty."

"Decision has already been made. Besides, you and Chelsea are the best team to protect her. We still haven't been able to locate Coby. I sent a SWAT team into NX5 headquarters, but he wasn't there. They have more secret locations than WITSEC, and he's most likely holed up in one of those until his orders are carried out."

"What orders?" Judah sat up straighter in his seat.

"Nelson questioned two of his members back at the department. There's a twenty-thousand-dollar hit on Sasha's head. Every assassin in the area will be aiming for her—not just Coby and his gang. If this Whitmore property is legit, then you need to get her there tonight."

Judah's chest tightened at the news. "I hear you. We'll move tonight. I'll be off the grid for a while after that. How do you want me to check in?"

"Use whatever communication the marshals deem fit. Chelsea will know how to get word to the right people." Taps from his sergeant's keyboard sounded through the phone. "Looks like the Whitmore property isn't in any of our databases. That's good. If we don't know about it, then assassins won't, either."

Judah noticed movement on the side of the porch and leaned forward. Sasha's mother walked toward him. She hugged a shawl around her shoulders with one hand and carried a small flashlight in the other. "I've got to go. Keep me and Chelsea updated on Nelson and Leila's progress however you can."

"Will do."

As he ended the call, Lila Kane tapped on the window. He pressed the button to lower the barrier between them. "Is everything okay?"

"I've got a pot of decaf coffee and some fresh-baked cookies that are hot out of the oven. I won't have my grandson's father sleeping in his truck tonight in wet clothes when I have a perfectly good couch."

Judah raised a hand. "That's not necessary. I am—"

"I didn't ask if it was necessary, and I won't take no for an answer. Finish up what you're doing here and head on inside. Everyone else is asleep, so no need to worry about making anyone uncomfortable. I'm guessing you have a change of attire somewhere in your SUV?"

"Yes, ma'am, I do."

"Good."

She turned and walked away before he had a chance to refuse. Judah figured she planned to talk to him about Bodie and Sasha, an inevitable occurrence when it came to the Kane family women. Ms. Lila was known around town for her strength of character and looking out for her girls.

He closed his laptop, grabbed his bag with clothes inside from the passenger seat and headed inside. Might as well have some hot coffee and homemade cookies before they headed out to a property he'd never heard of.

He slipped from the SUV and entered through the side door, trying to keep his movements as quiet as possible. Ms. Lila was not someone to keep waiting. He changed in the half bath right off the mudroom then made his way to the kitchen.

The scent of cinnamon permeated the room. Steam from

Lila's mug wisped next to a small plate holding four oat-meal raisin cookies. They looked delicious.

"Have a seat." Ms. Lila motioned to the chair opposite hers, and Judah sat. "I take it you like your coffee black?"

"Is there any other way?"

A slight smile curved on her lips, and she nodded. "I've always liked you, Judah. Not so much the way you acted after you lost your mom, but you always had an inner strength and conviction despite your other flaws."

He was surprised at her confession—he'd figured the woman wanted him nowhere near any of her daughters, much less being the father to her grandson.

She sat a filled coffee mug in front of him. "I'm going to share something with you that no one outside this family knows. God blessed me with five girls and no sons. I never knew why He didn't grant me a little boy, but now I have Bodie. You can understand how smitten I am with him."

She peered over the top of her mug and tapped one of the many silver rings decorating her fingers against the ceramic.

"I understand. I'm pretty smitten, too."

"Good, then we're on the same page. There's nothing I won't do to protect my girls or Bodie. That's why the good Lord put me on this earth, to take care of my family. I'd prayed my girls would choose a different career path, but they possessed too much of their father in them to end up anywhere besides law enforcement. I need to know what kind of danger we are in with this gang you call NX5."

He didn't want to scare the woman, but with the news of a bounty on Sasha's head, he also didn't want to su-garcoat the truth. Honesty was always the best policy in these situations. "The danger Sasha and Bodie are in is significant. NX5 will kill them if they can, and they will seek any means necessary to accomplish their goal. That is their pattern."

She stared at her coffee, then took a sip. "The Whitmore property Chelsea mentioned earlier is a piece of land my husband purchased years ago before he passed. It's on the other side of the mountain with a tunneled entrance that looks like a large rock face. Sasha knows how to open the gate. Once it closes, any hint of an entrance will disappear. As long as no one sees you enter, then you'll be hidden once you cross onto the land."

"I thought all that land belonged to the forestry service."

"Which is the way we want it. After my husband purchased the land, he pulled some strings to keep the property listed as private parkland on the maps. Once you drive through the rock tunnel, there's a small lot, then a bit of a hike to the bottom of the mountain. Sasha's dad built a residence into the side of the mountain—a modern retreat outfitted with everything you'll need to protect my daughter and grandson. You'll leave first thing in the morning."

"Actually, I think we need to leave tonight. I know she wanted to talk to the DA, but—"

"No need to worry about that. I'll meet with the DA and tell him about the man who attacked her. Surely DA Strut will understand why my daughter can't meet him in person. Going to the courthouse is a death sentence—I don't want her anywhere near the place. Plus, Bodie needs to be with his parents right now."

She reached out and patted his hand. "That includes you. Time to step up and be the father he needs."

Judah swallowed the last bite of cookie. "I plan to. I guess I'm just a little nervous about being a father."

"Every parent is nervous when it comes to their children. That never goes away. We learn to live with it and pray God keeps them safe. Your faith will guide you on how to be a good father."

"Not sure I have much faith in myself regarding fatherhood. I didn't grow up with a very good example."

"Then rely on God. He *is* good and loves you more than you love Bodie. You know that, right?"

Judah's heart began to race. He wasn't ready to have a conversation about what he knew about God, which wasn't much, except what he'd learned from a few vacation Bible school moments with friends. Time to change the topic. "When you say the home is outfitted with everything we'll need, what exactly do you mean?"

Ms. Lila drained the last of her coffee and placed the empty mug in the sink. "My husband was an FBI agent. He bought the Whitmore property as an off-grid place to get away from the stresses of his job. We've kept the living quarters modern and updated. In the primary bedroom, there's a floor-to-ceiling wall safe filled with ammunition and weapons, as well as a walk-in closet that doubles as a panic room. All of it is controlled by a keypad. Only my daughters and I can access the area. Underneath the rug in the den is a secret exit that takes you out through a network of tunnels that exit to the other side of the cave. Sasha knows the way, but don't go without her. One wrong turn and you'll never find the way out."

"No one outside the family knows about this place?" Judah handed her his empty mug and then leaned against the large island.

"My husband was a clever man, Detective. He set up an LLC and purchased the property so when people searched our family name the property wasn't connected. The registered owner is Greystone Holdings, LLC."

"Greystone?"

"A random selection. We made up the Whitmore name so there would be no ties back to us, but also so we would know which location we were discussing. This is not the only property my husband outfitted. He had multiple death threats on his head after dismantling several drug cartels' enterprises during his career."

"I never realized his work was so dangerous. He always seemed to be so calm."

"That's what made him such a good agent. I always expected we would need the place for him, considering the kind of cases he closed, but I never dreamed the property would be used for one of our girls. It's amazing how much foresight God gave him before his daughters were even grown. I tried to get them to go into health care, but they all chose some form of law enforcement like him. A father is one of the most influential people in a child's life."

Judah nodded, noting the not-so-subtle dig, and fought a yawn. The tug of sleep pulled at his body.

"Well, you certainly look like you could use some sleep. The couch is already dressed with clean sheets and a fresh pillow. You know where the downstairs bath is. Also, all my girls sleep with a gun nearby. Sasha and Bodie are in the middle room upstairs with armed sisters on each side. Their father taught them never to shoot until they knew the person was an intruder, however, I wouldn't go surprising anybody in the dark. That's a good way to get shot."

"I need to go wake them and head out."

"Might want to wait a couple of hours and get some shut-eye yourself. It's a long drive and a strenuous hike to the cabin. If you wake them before dawn, you'll still have time to make the trek in the dark."

He thanked her, and Ms. Lila headed off to bed. After a few moments, the house was quiet and Judah made his way into the large, open living room with vaulted ceilings. A nagging feeling came over him. Crime didn't sleep, and even a couple of hours would give them a head start on any NX5 assassins. Of course, they did have two police guards outside, so maybe a couple of hours wouldn't hurt. Sasha and Bodie were exhausted and needed rest.

The couch was comfortable, but he tossed and turned anyway, landing on his back to stare at the ceiling. Maybe if he counted the fan rotations, one after another, his mind would settle and allow sleep to come. He flipped to his side again and looked at the stairs. His two-year-old son was only one floor away, and Judah had never watched him sleep before. Was his face more angelic during the night than the day?

Only one way to find out.

Hardwood floors chilled the bottom of his feet as he slipped out from under the quilt Ms. Lila had given him. The stairs creaked once as he made his way up and entered the middle bedroom, closing the door behind him.

Sasha had her arm wrapped around their son and Bodie cuddled against her. His little boy's chest rose and fell with soft breathing, and Judah knew he'd never leave them again. He wasn't sure what that meant for his and Sasha's relationship, but he'd be there as long as she'd let him. The shock of fatherhood had subsided quickly after his initial meeting, and now all he wanted was to be a part of his son's life.

Judah sank into an armchair next to the bed. Sasha mumbled and rolled away from him, facing the wall. He tried to be still, not wanting to wake her or Bodie, but he couldn't leave just yet, either. A few more minutes wouldn't hurt.

With one swift movement, Sasha sat straight up, twisted

and pointed her gun at him. Judah pushed his palms into the air. "Don't shoot." He kept his voice low. "It's me."

She exhaled and dropped her arm. "It's not wise to sneak into someone's bedroom in the middle of the night. That's how people get shot."

"Sorry. I wasn't planning on you waking up."

"Has anyone ever told you it's kind of creepy to watch someone sleep?"

He looked at Bodie. "Can you blame me? He's perfect."

She followed his gaze, then scooted from the bed and returned her gun to the lockbox. "He is."

"How'd you get that thing out of there so quick?"

"It opens with my fingerprint. I heard you come in, and when I rolled over, I unlocked the lid and grabbed my gun."

"So you heard me?"

"I'm a light sleeper, especially these days." Sasha stepped over to the window, keeping her voice low. He figured she didn't want to wake Bodie. "Why are you in our room?"

A lone dog barked outside in the distance, drawing his attention to the perimeter of the property. Everything looked calm and serene, unlike the anxiety growing inside him as he tried to come up with the words to give her the latest update. "Coby put a bounty on your head. We need to move out tonight."

"This is small-town Shadow Creek, North Carolina. What exactly does that mean? Surely not that he's hired assassins?"

"Not hired, exactly, but offered a reward for the person who can prove they eliminated you."

She rubbed a hand across her forehead. "Goodness. That seems a bit extreme."

"NX5 has done this in the past. Offering a reward keeps

Coby from getting his hands dirty but still provides the results he needs."

"How very mafia-esque of him. And what about Bodie?"

Judah looked at his sleeping son. "We take him with us."

When he turned his gaze back to Sasha, a green laser swept across the room and landed on her chest.

His heart raced as he shoved her into the shadows, then lunged onto the bed, covering Bodie with his body. The child screamed and squirmed beneath him as gunfire sprayed through the room. Glass shattered and debris pelted his back as he pulled Bodie to the floor.

Sasha crawled over, grabbed her gun again, then reached for Bodie. "It's okay, baby. I'm here."

The little boy lunged for his mother, who pulled him into the bathroom. Judah followed.

"We need to get out of here." Sasha hugged her son tight with one hand, her weapon in the other.

"Agreed. What's the best exit, preferably hidden?"

"There isn't one." Sasha looked back into the room, where more gunfire erupted. She pulled in tight next to him, her body trembling against his. "This place isn't like the Whitmore property. There's no secret way out or panic rooms. We're gonna have to fight."

"I'll fight. You and Bodie get somewhere safe. They can't hurt you if they can't find you." Judah wasn't going to let anyone harm his family—even if he had to sacrifice his life to save them.

SIX

Sasha's sisters shouted commands through the house and returned a strong defensive counterassault against the intruders, keeping them from entering the home. Bodie sobbed against his mother's shoulder and tightened his hold on her neck. She had to get him out of here.

Chelsea flung open the opposite bathroom door that led into the hallway. "Follow me."

Her sister held an AR-15 in her hands and carried a nine-millimeter pistol on her hip. Sasha hunkered down behind her, holding Bodie in her arms while Judah took up the rear.

The back staircase exited into the kitchen, right outside the door that led to the basement. Chelsea rounded the corner to cover Sasha and Bodie as they made their way down the basement stairs.

Her sister fired several rounds at intruders who tried to enter through the front entrance. "Dani, you get the front."

"Covered."

Once they were clear, Chelsea locked the basement door and joined them.

She handed Sasha a pair of keys. "Take my Jeep." Chelsea rotated the assault rifle to her back and pulled the dusty tarp off a 1980s Wagoneer. "Go to the Whitmore property, and make sure no one follows you. I'll come tonight as soon as I make sure everything here is secure."

"Does this thing even run?" Sasha asked.

"Better than when it rolled off the factory floor and I've made some improvements to it."

"Like what?"

"Bulletproof glass, and I swapped out the motor for a Chevy LS engine with a new transmission. I'd planned to use it to transport witnesses back and forth to the courthouse for their testimonies and had to have the best of everything. You can take this about anywhere, including the Whitmore property. Now, time to get out of here. We have multiple teams coming from all sides of the property. Leila called in a SWAT team to help but they're three minutes away. When you drive out, you'll be attacked, so keep your head down."

She hugged her sister's neck. "You've got to get everybody out of here. Protect them, Chelsea."

"We've got this, now go."

With no more time to waste, Sasha carried Bodie to the passenger side of the vehicle, then turned and handed Judah the keys. "You drive. I'm gonna cover Bodie in the back. Do you know the way?"

"A general sense from what your mom told me. Just don't let me pass the entrance."

"I won't." Sasha climbed into the rear with her son and placed him on the seat. "Lie down here, Bodie. I've got you."

She stretched out beside him on the vinyl and braced herself for a rough ride.

Judah started the engine. "As soon as I open the garage door, they'll be on us. Stay down."

"I'm scared, Momma." Bodie's little body shook next

to hers. If only she hadn't gone to Hank's office, then her son would be in his bed right now, safe and sound, instead of escaping a barrage of bullets and murderous gang members. Their lives would be normal. This was far from anything a young child should have to experience.

She hugged him. "Stay close to me. We're going to be okay."

The words rang a bit hollow in her heart, not knowing the outcome of their dire situation, but her job as a mother was to protect him no matter what.

Judah pressed the garage door opener. "Here we go."

The Jeep lurched forward, and Sasha grabbed the back of the seat to keep her and Bodie from rolling into the floor. Bullets pinged off the metal sides as Judah shifted through the gears and swerved into the yard to dodge something or someone. Sasha kept her head down and her body over her son. They bounced in the back seat together as Judah raced down the long dirt road. The windows cracked but didn't shatter, thanks to the bulletproof glass her sister had installed. Dust swirled in through the vents and around the vehicle, making the number of gunmen hard to pinpoint. She didn't want to know. All she wanted was to get Bodie to safety.

Her son coughed.

Sasha pulled his pajama shirt up over his nose and mouth. "Is that better?"

Her little boy raised his big blue eyes to hers and nodded. She did the same with her shirt. "It's like we're cowboys escaping from the bad guys."

The corners of his eyes lifted. "I like cowboys."

"Me, too."

He snuggled tighter against her. "Love you, Momma."

She pressed her lips to the top of his head. "Love you, too, Bodie."

They remained low in the back until the gunfire subsided. The gravel road smoothed to asphalt, and Sasha raised up to look out the back window. The dark road behind them was vacant, and a forest of tall evergreen trees lined the sides. No one followed. She sat up and let Bodie stretch out to sleep.

"You've got about another half mile and then our turn will be on the left. Look for a tree shaped like a deer head, and then the large rock face will be on our left after that."

Sasha ran her fingers through her son's dark curls, thankful he was able to sleep after what they'd been through. They'd almost died tonight, and she closed her eyes for a moment, thanking God for His protection. They'd made it out alive. She'd never dreamed an army of assassins would invade her family's home and take aim at her son. Maybe WITSEC really was the best place for them to go.

Judah glanced in the rearview mirror. "Tree's up ahead, and I see the large rock. How do I open it?"

"Pull next to the trunk."

When he stopped, she rolled down her window and placed her hand into the rock's crevice. "There's a scanner inside that is only triggered by one of the Kane family's palm prints."

The rock slid open to the left and closed back up after they drove through. Her father had thought of everything when he constructed this property. He'd never told her of the times he used the location or why, but their mother would always have them pray for her dad when he was in dangerous situations.

"I never would've known this was a tunnel. Looks like real rock from the road."

"The surface pretty much is. Dad had the opening covered and fitted to blend in with the surroundings when it closed. He wanted everything about this place to be hidden. He had a sculptor create the design. No one has ever breached the gate since it was put in place."

With Bodie sleeping in the back seat and now that they were safely on the Whitmore property, Sasha climbed to the front beside Judah and rolled down the window. A warm summer wind blew across her body and provided a short reprieve from the aching exhaustion plaguing her muscles. All this because she was in the wrong place at the wrong time.

Several bullet holes dotted the hood, and one had pierced the windshield. "I thought she said the windshield was bulletproof."

"It was, mostly, but I guess some bullets are made to pierce the glass."

Sasha followed the trajectory to Judah's right arm, lying limp in his lap. Something dark covered his skin. She turned in her seat and noted the stained sleeve of his T-shirt. "Have you been shot?" She pulled up the cloth, and he flinched.

"It's nothing."

"You have. We need to get you to the hospital."

"The bullet grazed the side of my arm but no major damage. We can't go to the hospital, anyway. NX5 will find you and Bodie if we do."

He was right. All hospitals required patients to be recorded in the electronic medical record, and even though HIPAA laws punished those who dared to do an unlawful search, large bribes or threats could sometimes convince employees to provide information with a few keystrokes. The hospital was out except for major emergencies.

Instead, she pulled off her outer T-shirt and tied it around his wound. "That should help slow down the bleeding until we get inside. There's a fully stocked medical cabinet at the cabin. We'll clean and bandage your arm when we get there."

The long driveway wound deep into the woods, over a small creek and then widened into a dirt parking area that needed a trim. Her family liked the place to look overgrown and abandoned. Judah pulled up to the dilapidated split-rail fence and cut the engine. "I thought there was a cabin here."

Sasha climbed in the back and picked up Bodie. "It's another mile hike down the path."

"What path?"

"Exactly." Sasha smiled when she stepped from the Jeep, pulled out her phone and punched in the coordinates on her digital compass. "Follow me. I know the way."

After fifteen minutes of traipsing through thick mountain laurels, one briar patch and a couple of abandoned spider webs, Sasha stood at the top of a steep embankment. Her arms burned with the exertion of carrying Bodie such a long way. She aimed her phone's light over the edge, trying to see into the black abyss below. "The cabin's at the bottom."

"And how do you propose we get down there in the middle of the night?"

Bodie started to squirm, and Sasha lowered his feet to the ground. "There's a system of ropes and lines that we'll use."

Sasha motioned to Bodie. "Come on, bud. You can lean against my legs and hold on to the rope, okay?"

"Why don't you let me carry him? I'm used to carrying fifty-pound backpacks for hunting trips. I think I can handle a twenty-five-pound toddler."

"What about your arm?"

Judah looked at her homemade bandage, now stained red. "My arm's okay. Nothing but a scratch."

"Be honest. If it hurts too much, then I'll have him lean against me and walk down." The last thing she wanted was a hero right now. She needed the truth and the assurance her son would be okay.

He smiled and knelt in front of Bodie. "Can you hold on real tight to my neck? If you do, I'll take you on a piggyback ride."

Dark curls bounced as her son nodded. Sasha helped him into place, then moved around and faced him. Bodie rested his head on Judah's shoulder. "You think he'll hold on the entire trek down? It is a pretty steep decline, and I don't want him to let go."

"Then use my belt to secure him to me." Judah unfastened the buckle and pulled the strap of leather from the loops, handing it to Sasha. "This should keep him in place."

"And your pants?"

"They fit just fine. I got used to wearing a belt on patrol and can't go without one now."

Sasha stretched out the length and held it up to him. "You think it will reach?"

"Are you calling me fat?" he teased.

Fat was not a word she'd use to describe Judah's toned body. The man had to spend at least five days a week in the gym with a physique like his.

"Of course not." Heat flushed her face, and she was thankful for the dark.

Her fingers grazed the ridges of muscle as she circled the belt around him and tightened it into place. His gaze weighed heavy on her as she slid the last bit through the buckle in front.

"How's that?"

He placed his hand over hers. "Can you go one tighter without squeezing Bodie too much?"

More warmth flushed into her cheeks, and she hesitated. He used to hold her hand when they'd dated. His touch was light and gentle, remaining there for a moment longer than needed. She unbuckled the belt, cinched the clasp one notch tighter and tried to catch her breath. "There. Better?"

"Perfect."

But his gaze wasn't on the buckle. He was looking at her, first her eyes, then her lips. His fingers rose to her cheek and tipped her chin. He didn't kiss her, but she wouldn't have stopped him.

"I'm so sorry, Sasha. For all I put you through back in the day. You were right. I didn't handle my father abandoning us or my mother's sickness well, and I turned to alcohol instead of leaning on the ones who love me...loved me."

His words, long overdue, pulled at her heart. The pain he put her through during his addiction had almost destroyed her, and for him to acknowledge his part in the demise of their relationship brought healing.

He continued, "I don't think I've ever apologized to you, and I should have. Please know that most of the harsh words I said during those times were not how I felt. I just didn't know how to handle everything I was going through. I'd lost my dad and my mom, and then you left, too."

Sasha took his hand in hers. "I understand. I never should've kept Bodie a secret. Even though we weren't together, you had a right to know, and I should've told you sooner."

She dropped her gaze to the ground. Memories surfaced

in her mind and confused her determination not to fall for Judah Walker again. She had to keep her focus and make sure the decisions she made to keep Bodie safe weren't clouded by a rekindled romance. Especially if she decided to enter Witness Protection and he didn't come with them. Her heart couldn't take the pain of losing him again. Best if they kept things platonic and as uncomplicated as possible.

Besides, the last time she let her guard down and gave in to temptation, she'd ended up pregnant with Bodie. He was a gift, of course, but she wanted her next child to be born into a committed marriage. She had to be strong and resist the chemistry between them.

She released his hand and pressed hers against Judah's chest. "Whatever you do, don't drop our son." She moved around to his back and made sure Bodie was secure, placing a small kiss against his cheek.

"I promise I won't let go," Judah said.

"Giddy-up, horsey." Bodie gave a little bounce on his back.

"Get ready, cowboy. This horse is headed back to the barn."

Bodie giggled.

"You're sure your arm is okay?" Sasha worried his injury would cause fatigue.

"I'm fine. Now let's get down there so we can get some rest and food. I'm starved."

Sasha moved to the edge of the steep bank and reached for the rope tied to a tree, trying not to think about the sheer danger they were facing. "I'll go first. Let me get to the next line before you start. We upgrade the ropes every couple of years, but I'd feel better with only one person's weight on them at a time."

"Makes sense. Ladies first." Judah extended a hand and

helped her get her footing, then stepped back to watch her steps.

"Use as many of the root holds as you can. They will secure your descent."

Sasha wrapped the rope around her waist and leaned back, testing the strength. Stable. She looked below her into the darkness of the drop. A sliver of moonlight cut through the trees and cast a dim glow to the bottom, thirty feet down. Nothing like hiking almost blind to get the adrenaline pumping.

The first step over the edge was always the hardest. She leaned back and dropped a couple of feet. Maybe this wouldn't be so hard after all and within thirty minutes they'd all be sleeping soundly in their beds.

Another step. Then two.

She settled into a groove and made the descent to the next rope. "All clear."

Maybe she should wait for Judah to crest over the embankment, just to make sure he didn't have any trouble. Visions of her son coming unbuckled and plunging down the mountainside plagued her thoughts. She was being silly. Judah wouldn't let anything happen to Bodie.

She grabbed the next line, placed her foot against a root and leaned back. The rope snapped.

Sasha screamed.

Wind whipped around her body as she fell backward. Dust swirled and rocks shifted underneath her. She grasped for any hold, but her fingers caught nothing except thin air. Everything around her slowed and sped up at the same time. Rocks and trees slammed against her but did little to decrease her momentum. She continued to roll. Pain shot up her side and back. Judah yelled her name, but she couldn't breathe to answer him.

Sasha rolled straight for the staircase her father had built. The wooden landing came fast and her head and upper body struck the post, stopping her decline. A sheet of black edged into her vision with only one name on her mind as unconsciousness overtook her.

Bodie.

Bark cut into Judah's palms as he descended the steep grade, holding on to limbs and planting each foot with care. He had to get to Sasha, but he also had to make sure he and his son didn't fall. The snap of her rope replayed in his mind, and the moon's glow highlighted the terror in her face as she fell.

Please, God, don't let her be dead.

The last time he'd prayed was after his father left and then again when his mother got cancer but God didn't answer his prayers the way he wanted. He'd stopped asking God for anything in his life but not knowing if Sasha was dead or alive forced a desperate plea.

Bodie's little hands pressed against his throat. What if he hadn't offered to carry him down? Judah almost felt sick at the thought. Sasha had to be okay. He was barely ready to be a father, much less tackle raising a child without her. Bodie adored his mother—and if Judah was honest, so did he.

"Momma slide?"

"Something like that." Judah continued making sure to plant each foot with care. He fought his instinct to cry out for her again or let the panic rush his descent. He had to stay calm for Bodie. His foot slipped, sending loose rocks and dirt tumbling down the hill. He caught himself against a tree and paused for a moment, listening. Nothing but cicadas chirping an annoying song. He started again.

"Judah?" Sasha's voice was music to his ears.

"I'm almost there. Are you hurt?"

"Banged up pretty good. How's Bodie?"

"I ride a horsey, Momma."

Sasha laughed. "Ow. That hurts."

"What hurts?" A few more steps and Judah reached the top of the landing, the only level area about three-fourths of the way down the steep mountainside. Evergreen trees surrounded them, and one final staircase descended in front of him to the grassy flat area where the cabin was located next to a bold stream.

Sasha sat on the wooden planks. "Everything, especially my ribs and ankle." She tried to stand and grabbed for his shoulder to steady her gait. "And I'm dizzy."

"Just stay where you are. We can wait a few minutes until you get your bearings. Looks like you hit your head."

"Yeah. The post didn't like me plowing into it." She touched the gash and pulled back stained, shaky fingertips.

He prayed she didn't have a severe concussion, but after a fall like that, he'd be surprised if she didn't. "Looks like we'll both be needing your mom's medicine cabinet."

Bodie wiggled on Judah's back. "Down."

"Is that the cabin down there?" he asked.

Sasha nodded to the stairs in front of them. "Yeah. You can see a bit of the roof through the trees right over there. To the left of the stairs."

Judah unbuckled the belt and helped Bodie to his feet. The little boy toddled over to his mother and hugged her. "Momma okay?"

"I'm going to be just fine." She kissed Bodie's cheek, then looked at Judah. "Can you help me walk?"

He wrapped a hand around her waist, and she leaned against his side. Her curves had always fit nicely against him. She wasn't too short or tall but tucked right into his arms. He fought the urge to sweep her into his arms and carry her the rest of the way. She wouldn't want that, especially after she'd pulled away when he apologized earlier. He figured a move like that might backfire and remind her of all his past mistakes. He'd made plenty of them during their relationship. If only he could get back what he never should've let go.

With each step, she limped a bit more.

"Sprained ankle?" he asked.

"Most likely. I don't think it's broken, but it hurts."

"Try not to put too much weight on it. You can lean against me more if you need to."

"I'm good."

They reached the bottom of the staircase and walked across the grass to the front door, where Sasha entered the code. Judah helped her inside, lowering her to the couch and placed a pillow underneath her foot. Bodie climbed up beside her. Judah could only hope that his son might cuddle next to him like that one day, too.

He crossed the room into the kitchen and found an ice pack in the freezer, then handed it to Sasha. "Here. This will help."

"I do it." Bodie scrambled down off the couch and placed the pack on his mother's ankle. "Good, Momma?"

"Very good, sweet boy." She touched Judah's hand, and he stilled. "We need to clean your arm."

He glanced at the T-shirt that was no longer white tied around his wound. "It'll be okay for a few more minutes."

His body was exhausted, and he sank into a leather club chair beside her, resting his head back. "We should be safe here. I doubt anyone will think to look at the bottom of the mountain we just descended."

"Agreed."

Dim light from the morning sunrise streaked into the room. They'd been through so much that time seemed to have skipped several days. Now all he wanted was some sleep, a shower and something to eat. He figured Sasha felt the same way.

Bodie toddled over to a box of cars located in the TV cabinet, selected a truck and brought it to him. "It's broken. Fix it."

Judah snapped the wheel back into place, held out the toy and tousled his son's hair. "There you go. Good as new."

Bodie smiled and climbed up into the chair beside him. "You go fast."

The little boy rolled the car up the arm of the chair and made a zoom sound.

"I wanted to get you and your mom to a safe place, so I had to go fast."

"No more bad guys." A serious expression clouded Bodie's face, and Judah looked at Sasha before responding. He didn't want to agree, not knowing if Coby would find them again, but he also didn't want to scare the child any more than he already had.

As if on cue, Sasha leaned forward. "Judah and I are never going to let anything happen to you. You're safe now. You hear me?"

He nodded.

"Good." Sasha stood, a little slower than normal, and held out her hand to their son. "What do you say about seeing if that truck will float?"

Bodie's eyes lit up. "Yeah. Truck float."

"I'm going to give him a bath. Meet you back here in fifteen? We'll take care of your arm then."

"I'm more concerned about the injuries you have from

the fall. Why don't you let me give him a bath while you go lie down?"

"I'm just a little bruised up, but I promise to rest later." She led their son toward a hallway. "You should poke your head in. Bodie loves his baths, and he's quite funny when he gets to splashing in the water. I think we might have a little swim bug on our hands. I'd hoped to get him some lessons at the community center this summer, but with moving back home and now this, I guess we'll have to put that off for a while."

"Things will get back to normal, I promise. These precautions are only temporary."

"I know." She pointed toward the other end of the home. "The other bedrooms are that way. Extra clothes are in all the closets, along with a survival backpack if we need to make a quick getaway. And bring the first aid kit from the hall bath. Just because you think your arm is fine doesn't mean it is."

Bodie tugged her toward the hallway and they disappeared around the corner.

After showering, Judah found the extra clothes and the backpack, then headed to the hall bath. A large wall of cabinetry held every kind of medical supply anyone needed—from IV bags to painkillers and surgical disappeared. He grabbed the ACE bandages for Sasha's ankle, medical tape and disinfectant, then returned to the living area. She had curled up on the couch with her hair still wet and fallen asleep.

He hated to wake her, but after the night they'd had and the fact that his arm was killing him, he really wanted to get things wrapped up.

"Sash." He gently shook her shoulder.

Her eyes lifted, and she sat up. Judah took a seat beside her. "Is Bodie sleeping?"

"I could barely keep him awake in the tub. He didn't even try to get up when I put him in the bed." She lifted up Judah's shirtsleeve and let out a slow whistle. "This looks infected."

"I found some penicillin in the closet. I'll take it to be safe."

"There's some good pain meds in there, too."

He raised his other hand. "I don't like to take anything I can't buy over the counter. Not with my history."

"Right. I guess that's wise."

"I don't know about wise, but definitely necessary." He flinched when she placed the cleaning sponge on his wound. "Sorry. It's cold."

Sasha cleaned and bandaged his injury, then gathered up all the wrappers. "I hope Bodie doesn't have nightmares. He's exhausted, but after all he's been through I wouldn't be surprised."

She was a good mother. Always making sure their son had everything he needed. "Even if he does, we'll be there for him. You don't have to do this by yourself anymore."

He motioned for her to take a seat on the couch and lifted her ankle to his lap. "Are you sure it's not broken? It's twice the size of the other one."

"I've sprained it before. Tore the ligaments. It's painful but should start going down in a few days. If it doesn't improve, then maybe we can get an X-ray or something."

He removed the ACE bandage from the box and started at the ball of her foot, wrapping the area twice to get a snug fit. "Is that too tight?"

She shook her head. "Feels good." Her cheeks flushed pink as he kept wrapping, adding extra support around the ankle area, and moved up her leg to secure it. "There. Better?"

"Much."

He didn't move her legs from his lap, and she reclined on a pillow and watched him as he crumpled the box in his hand. "I guess we need to discuss our next steps."

"For today, we're going to stay here, and as long as NX5 doesn't locate us, then this will be the best place for us unless you decide to take my advice and go into WITSEC."

"After last night, I think that might be the best, but then again, we'd always be looking over our shoulders, and Bodie would never have the love of his aunts and grandma around him. That would be the true trauma."

"Maybe so, but he'd be alive." He placed the box on the coffee table and would toss it later.

"And far away from you. Is that what you want? Because if it is, then I can get one of my sisters to stay with us. You don't have to be in our lives."

A tinge of anger permeated her tone, and she repositioned herself on the couch, moving her legs to the coffee table.

"Of course not. I'm just trying to think of what's best for our son."

"And you don't think I am? I've been taking care of Bodie far longer than you, and everything I do is in his best interest."

"Except telling him about his father."

His words seemed to punch the air right out of the room. Clearly the secret still festered underneath his calm demeanor despite her apology. Pain etched into the lines of her face, and she stood and stepped back, making him regret the words.

"I apologized. What more can I do? I can't go back and change the decisions I made. Are you ever going to be able to forgive me? I get that you're angry and need more time to process everything, but if we keep taking swipes at each other, then parenting together is never going to work."

"I know. I'm trying. This isn't easy."

"Life never is."

"Tell me about the custody agreement you and Hank put together. That might help."

She sat back down and readjusted the pillows on the couch. "Maybe this isn't the best time. We're both exhausted, and I can't think clearly when I'm tired. Let's go to bed and try again in a few hours."

Judah watched her disappear behind her bedroom door, then rested his head back on the couch and stared at the vaulted ceilings. Here he was again—watching the fan whirl, counting the rotations.

He closed his eyes and wished that conversation had gone differently. Sasha was an amazing mother, and he admired her. But the news of his son had triggered a protective instinct he'd never realized he had. He only wanted to make sure they lived a safe life. He could join them at a later date, after Hank's killer was behind bars. He wanted to be available in case Nelson and Leila needed him. He'd never be able to be the kind of father he wanted to be for Bodie until Hank's murder was solved.

The sun stretched its rays right into Judah's eyes. From the position, the time had to be around noon. He sat up on the couch and dropped his feet onto the hardwood floors. The house was quiet. Not even a peep from Sasha and Bodie's room. He hoped they were sleeping well, since they seemed to have escaped the threat. For now.

He stood and shuffled to the kitchen. Despite the lunchtime hour, he needed coffee. Black and strong.

Eggs and yogurt were in the refrigerator with good dates, and he found some bacon in the freezer. Seemed like Lila Kane's theory of always being prepared for company extended to their wooded retreat as well.

The coffee made a loud noise as the brewing stopped and the heavy scent permeated the room. If Sasha was as light a sleeper as she said, then the scents of bacon, eggs and coffee would wake her up.

Judah filled up his mug and inhaled. Nothing like a strong cup of joe to get the mental juices flowing. Sasha tiptoed from her room and closed the door behind her. "Morning. Coffee?"

Judah glanced at the clock. "I've got coffee but it's after noon, not morning."

"Good. Then we got at least six hours sleep. That's good."

He found another mug, rinsed it and poured her a cup. "Sorry. I was trying to be quiet and not wake you, but my body needed some caffeine and food. I couldn't wait any longer."

"You never need to apologize for making coffee." She flashed a smile before taking a long sip.

"How's your ankle?"

She held out her foot, still wrapped from earlier. "I think the swelling has gone down some, so that's a good sign."

She moved to his side and pushed up his shirtsleeve. Her gentle touch sent a chill up his arm. "Looks like the bleeding's stopped, and the wound isn't red around the edges anymore."

He rotated his shoulder a bit. "It feels better."

"Good." She took another sip of her coffee but didn't move away from his side. He'd forgotten how beautiful she looked with a fresh face and her hair swept up into a messy bun on the top of her head. She still wore the wrinkled T-shirt and shorts from last night. What he wouldn't give to kiss her, but she'd probably smack him if he tried anything like that. After seeing her with Bodie, the least he could do was respect her decision and her faith in God, even if he didn't share it.

He moved to the other side of the island and took a seat, hoping a bit of distance would cool down his thoughts.

Something thumped against the outside of the cabin, and Sasha straightened. "What was that?"

Judah placed his mug on the countertop, put a finger to his lips and pulled his gun from the holster where he'd left it on the shelf earlier. He'd kept it up high so Bodie would have no way to reach the weapon.

Sasha moved back to the bedroom and peeked in the door, then looked back to Judah. "Wasn't Bodie. He's still asleep."

The basement staircase creaked with the weight of footsteps, and Judah placed his hand on the knob, ready for any intruder. Before anyone could reach the main level, he pulled open the door and aimed his weapon.

Hands raised into the air. "Don't shoot. It's me, Chelsea."

Judah stepped back so she could enter, and Sasha rushed over and gave her sister a hug. "I'm so glad you're okay. Everyone else is, too, right?"

Chelsea shot Judah a grave look over her sister's shoulder. She pulled back and took Sasha's hands in hers. "I've got some bad news. Mom's been shot, and she's in the ICU."

Sasha's face paled. "Is she going to be okay?"

"The next twenty-four hours will tell us for sure, but we're praying she will be."

"This is all my fault. I never should've come back to Shadow Creek."

"Don't say that. Mom was so happy to have you and Bodie back home. This is not your fault. She's got the best doctors and nurses taking care of her. They've got her in a medically induced coma to give her body time to heal."

"What happened?"

"After you left, we thought all the intruders were gone. Mom stepped out on the porch to check on the dog, and a sniper shot a round across the field. They hit her in the shoulder, and it nicked one of the main arteries. Thankfully, the cops and an ambulance were on-site by then. They rushed her to the hospital, took her to surgery, and the doctor said everything went well, but a few days will tell us more."

"I need to see her." Sasha stood and was headed back toward her bedroom when Judah reached out for her hand.

His heart broke for her. "You can't go."

"Try and stop me." She pulled her hand from his.

"Judah's right, sis. A trip to the hospital is too dangerous for you and for Bodie. Coby will be expecting you to show up. He'll send some of his gang, and they won't hesitate to put a bullet between your eyes, plus you'll put a whole host of other people in danger. You saw what it was like last night. That was a war zone, and you don't want to take that into a hospital."

She turned to Judah. "Can't you pull some strings and set up a way for me to get into the hospital to see her? Keep me undercover somehow?"

"The way these guys came after us last night, I don't think hospital security can handle something like that."

Sasha swiped the tears streaking her cheeks and went to her bedroom without another word. He hated to disappoint her and keep her from visiting her mom. Maybe he could come up with a plan to sneak her inside. He did have connections at the hospital who could help him. Judah poured another cup of coffee.

"Got a mug for me?" Chelsea asked.

"Sure." He retrieved a cup and filled it to the top. "I hope you like it black."

"Is there any other way?"

He smiled. "I said the same thing to your mom last night."

"That's a good way to win her over."

He took another sip. "Looks like I'm not doing so good with your sister."

Chelsea's gaze landed on Sasha's closed bedroom door. "She's had some hard knocks in life. You of all people should know that, but she loves that little boy of yours, and she loves her family. She'll do whatever it takes to protect them."

"Can't blame her there."

He looked out the window. A clear-cut opening in the trees provided a view of the layered mountains, a glimpse of the bold river at the bottom of the hill and, in the far distance, miles above them, a dirt service road. The one they'd taken after crossing onto the Whitmore property. A reflection caught his eye.

"Did your dad have some binoculars?"

"Yeah." Chelsea crossed the room, opened a drawer and handed him a pair. "Why?"

Judah raised them to his face. "Looks like we've got company."

He handed the binoculars to Chelsea for a view. "Any reason why someone would be on the only road that winds up to the abandoned parking area above the cabin?"

She handed him back the glasses. "No one but my family should be on that road, and none of us have a van. They're miles away, though, and they still have the hike in. Could be hours, if they even find the place."

"I'm not willing to take any chances."

He crossed to Sasha's door and knocked. She didn't answer. He tried the handle, and the door opened. "Sash, we've got to—"

Bodie was still sleeping on the bed, but she wasn't in the room. The bathroom door was open and it was empty. He crossed to the bed and found a note.

Take care of Bodie. I have to visit my mom. I'm sorry.

Judah wadded the paper up in his fist and looked in the closet. The survival pack was gone.

Chelsea entered the room behind him. "Where's Sasha? We need to head out now."

He faced her and tossed her the wadded-up note. "We've got bigger problems."

SEVEN

Sasha stood at the railing of the private porch off her bedroom and stared out into the wooded forest around her. She jangled her sister's car keys in her hand. What was she thinking? She couldn't leave Bodie. He needed her right now more than anything, but she wanted to go see her mom. Why did life have to be so complicated? Tears streaked down her cheeks. Her mother would tell her to stay with her child and not worry about her, but how could she not worry? The woman who had raised and nurtured her was fighting for her life.

If only she hadn't come home. If she had stayed in Raleigh, then her mom wouldn't be lying in a hospital bed with machines helping her breathe and Sasha wouldn't be stuck in the middle of nowhere trying to keep her son safe.

The patio door behind her swung open, and Judah rushed out, a frantic look in his eyes.

"Don't worry. I'm still here. I couldn't leave."

He glanced back over his shoulder. "Chelsea. I found her." He pulled the door to and leaned against the wall, the weight of his stare penetrating her peripheral vision, but he remained silent. Probably too angry to speak.

"I'm sorry if I scared you. I had a weak moment and

really wanted to go see my mom. I know it sounds stupid, but—"

He held up his hand. "It's not stupid. You're worried about her, like any good daughter would be."

"I'm not a good daughter. I'm the black sheep of the family. The only one who broke the rules and got pregnant outside of marriage. I'm the one who left my family and stayed away for three years, keeping her grandson from her. If only I'd been stronger."

"This isn't all on you. I'm partly to blame also." He took a step closer. "But you can't go out there on your own. It's really dangerous and Bodie needs you, too. He's our priority now."

The door opened behind them again, and Chelsea stepped onto the deck, carrying Bodie. She shot Sasha a narrowed look. "What were you thinking?"

Bodie reached for Sasha, who took him into her arms. "I'm worried about Mom."

"We all are, and we're worried about you and Bodie, too. Don't go making things even worse." She moved back to the door. "I'll give you two a minute."

Sasha pressed her lips against the soft, smooth skin of Bodie's cheek, and he placed his sleepy head on her shoulder.

Judah ran his fingers across their son's back. "This little boy right here feels the exact same way about you that you feel about your mother. Imagine if he had to live life without you. It's normal to want to go see your mom, but she'd want you to be here with us, out of harm's way."

"I know." She understood his concern, but her heart was torn. "I keep thinking about her, lying in a hospital bed fighting for her life because of me. I can't sit around anymore, hiding and waiting for NX5 to find us. I thought I'd go to the hospital, sneak in and see her for a few minutes, then come back here. I know. Sounds ridiculous when I say it out loud."

Bodie hugged her neck tighter and clutched his blanket in his fist. He was always sleepy when he first woke up. She loved the extra cuddles he gave her.

"Ridiculous or not, my first priority is to keep you and Bodie safe. I can't do that if you're not here."

"That's why I'm still standing on the deck. I couldn't leave him."

Judah's phone vibrated, and he tapped through a couple of screens. "I connected to your father's cameras. Looks like we might've been compromised, and if so we need to head out before they reach the house. There's movement on the service road, and I'm not taking any chances."

Sasha walked back inside. "We can get a better view from Dad's security monitors in his office. Then we'll know if it's a threat or just some hikers who happened upon the property. If they're on the service road, then they are at least another hour away, plus the hike they have to make to the cabin is a good forty-five minutes."

"How's your ankle?"

Sasha held it out and pulled up the leg of her jeans. "Not as painful, but it might slow us down if we have to hike out of here. At least we have the lower exit off the property and won't have to head back up the mountain to where we entered. We don't come in that way because it's five miles longer."

"But it's flat?"

"Flatter than the first route. It runs down by the river."

She hoped her ankle would hold up. The swelling had gone down, and even though the muscles were sore, she was able to walk. A little slower than normal, but she'd do what she had to do to make sure to keep her son safe.

Bodie raised up and gave her a kiss on the cheek, and she nuzzled her nose against him. "You're the sweetest boy in the whole world."

"Cereal."

He reached toward the cabinet when she walked through the kitchen. "How about a Pop-Tart?"

Bodie clapped his hands. Chelsea reached for him. "I got him, sis. You go on and show Judah the cameras."

"Thanks."

Sasha pulled Chelsea's car keys from her pocket and placed them back on the bar. Her sister looked at them, then to her.

"I swiped them earlier."

Chelsea took the keys and shoved them into her pocket, then dug into the cabinets for Bodie's breakfast tart. "You always were the sneaky one. I'll make sure to be more diligent from now on."

Sasha led Judah down a long hallway to her father's office door and punched in a code on the keypad for entry. Inside, the space looked like a small war room, with multiple computers and four screens along the back wall. She powered everything up and logged into the camera footage. At least sixteen cameras were stationed throughout the property. "I don't see anything at the moment. We've got some time. Maybe it was a wild animal or some hikers who got off the beaten path."

"Maybe." Judah rolled out a chair and searched the screens in front of him. "I just don't want to take any chances. Seems like Coby always figures out where we are, and I can't figure out how. He must have someone on the inside."

"Wouldn't put it past him. The man's got connections across the entire Southeast."

Judah sat back and faced her. "You know this is what's best for you and Bodie, right? Hiding can seem passive, but until we have a better handle on the extent of Coby's orders, we have to lay low."

"Of course. I might not like being isolated from everyone I love, but I'll do everything in my power to protect our son. I just can't help feeling responsible for all this. Mom's in the ICU because of me. What if she…" The grim thought stole the rest of her words.

He took her hand in his. "I understand what you're going through. The idea of losing a parent, especially your mother, is hard. I know I didn't handle it well and turned to alcohol to deal with the pain."

"But you've done so well with your recovery." She ran a thumb across his knuckles.

"I'm not recovered. I'll always be an alcoholic, Sasha. The moment I forget that fact is the moment I'll pick up the bottle again, and I don't ever want to go back."

She kept quiet as he continued.

"But the one thing I did do right was spending time with my mom when she was sick, and you should be able to do the same." He pulled out his phone. "Let me see what I can do. Maybe there's a way to help you get in to see your mother and still keep NX5 in the dark. I've got some friends in the hospital that might be able to help sneak you in."

"And what about Bodie?"

"Chelsea can keep him. Who better to leave him with than an excellent US marshal?"

Her face brightened. "That might work. And my father kept some disguises in the hall closet. I think there's a blond wig in there along with some faux facial hair for you."

"I'll pass on the fake mustache, but the wig might not be a bad idea for you. I've always wanted to see you as a blonde."

She playfully slapped at his shoulder. "What is it with men and blondes?"

His smile faded. "This will still be highly dangerous. If Coby finds out what we're up to, then he could ambush us at the hospital, and they don't have the security to keep us safe. I'll arrange some undercover officers to help us, but are you sure you want to go through with it?"

Sasha nodded. "I need to see her."

Judah ran a hand through his hair. "I know you do, but I was hoping you'd agree to stay hidden. Anyway, I'll get a plan together and let Sergeant Quinn know. He'll have to approve the extra security details inside the hospital."

"Thanks. After this, I'll go wherever you think is best." She looked back at the monitor screens. "Looks like the earlier alarm was a false one. I don't see anyone on Dad's cameras."

"Are there any blind spots?"

"Not once you hit the service road. He has the entire perimeter covered." She zoomed in on one of the images. "Nope. Just a deer. You think we can make the trek today?"

"Yeah. Let me make a couple of phone calls and then we'll go. And don't forget about the disguise. It will help."

After a couple of hours of making phone calls and setting up surveillance with the precinct, they hiked the lower exit route down by the river and had Dani, her youngest sister, pick them up. They dropped Dani off at Lila's house, and then Sasha and Judah made the drive into town. He circled the hospital and parked in an isolated ambulance bay.

Sasha unbuckled her seat belt and reached for the door handle, but Judah touched her arm. "Wait. I need to make sure we have a clear path inside."

He stepped out and crossed to a secured door. The glass slid open, and Dr. Singer, the medical examiner, joined him. She placed something in Judah's hand and handed him a bag, then disappeared back inside the building while he rejoined Sasha.

"What did she give you?"

He held a white entry key card between his fingers. "Our way in. Dr. Singer has access to almost every department in the hospital. She's agreed to let us use an entrance reserved for doctors and gave us access to the ICU elevators. She told us we need to wear these."

Judah pulled out two white lab coats embroidered with a doctor's name and two surgical caps. He handed her a green one, which she fit into place over her blond wig then turned to him. "Can I pass for a surgeon?"

"Maybe an actor on a medical drama series."

"Very funny."

He slipped on his coat. "When we get in there, do exactly as I say. We can't take any chances on keeping you and your mom safe. There are a few plainclothes officers keeping an eye out for us, and we have hospital security on alert." He positioned a comms device in his ear. "They'll let us know if we have trouble."

Sasha waited as Judah checked his weapon and texted a few more messages, then they made their way inside and up to the ICU. He steered her away from the nurses' desk and down a back hallway, keeping an eye out for anything out of the ordinary.

The building was huge, with long corridors and patient rooms on both sides. Tiled floors shined from a recent polish, and photographs of local tourist destinations hung on the walls. The smell of antiseptic cleaners assaulted her nose, but she figured that was better than other medical scents. Another nurses' station was coming up on their right when Judah stopped her in front of room B503 and slid open the door.

Sasha pulled back the interior curtain and stepped inside.

A cacophony of beeps mixed with clicks and rhythmic breathing sounds from the ventilator greeted her upon entry. Sunlight streamed across the bed where a white sheet draped her mother's legs. She looked frail, with plastic wires attached in multiple places. Tubes extended from multiple areas, and Sasha lifted her gaze to the heart rhythm running across a display above the bed. Large numbers revealed normal oxygen saturation levels, pulse and blood pressure.

Sasha eyed the variety of intravenous bags infusing a plethora of medication into her mom's body. She moved to her bedside and slid her fingers into her mother's limp hand, kissing her cold knuckles. "I'm so sorry, Momma. If not for me, you wouldn't be here. You'd be home playing with Bodie or out riding horses."

She stared at her mother's face, hoping for any kind of response—a lash flutter or eyebrow scrunch—but she remained unmoving. Sasha had never faced the idea of life without her mother, but this forced her to consider all the grave outcomes. Her mom was her rock, the one she turned to when there was nowhere else to go. *Dear God, please don't let her die. I need her.*

Judah moved to the door and slid it open. "There's someone who wants to talk with you."

A man dressed in scrubs with a stethoscope around his

neck walked into the room. Gray streaked the sides of his hair, and he gave her a slight smile when he entered. "I'm Dr. Kyle, your mom's surgeon. She's doing well and should make a full recovery."

"So she's going to be okay?"

"As long as her vitals hold and she keeps getting stronger then we're headed in the right direction. She's a fighter and we're keeping her sedated for now to give her body time to heal. We hope to start weaning her off the ventilator in a couple of days."

"How extensive are her injuries? I know she was shot, but how much damage did it do?"

"She was shot in the shoulder and had a pneumothorax—or air in the lung cavity. This makes breathing a challenge, but we were able to fix that in the ER."

"Then why did she need surgery?"

"The bullet nicked her subclavian artery, which runs horizontal from the neck under the clavicle and over to the arm. We were able to repair the injury but she lost a good amount of blood. We gave her a couple of transfusions and that's why we are keeping her in the ICU. So far she's responding well."

"That's good news." Sasha wiped away the tears and turned back to her mother, ignoring the buzz of her phone in her pocket. "You're going to be out of here and back home in no time."

Judah placed a hand on her shoulder. "I don't mean to rush you, but we need to wrap things up."

"We just got here."

"Nelson texted. They intercepted NX5 members at the main entrance, but there could be others in the building. One of the guys had a janitor's badge, which would give him access to multiple areas in the hospital. If others have the same, then they could be headed in our direction. We need to get you out of here."

"Can't he arrest them or something?"

"They been removed from the premises, but we can't be sure there aren't more already inside."

Sasha wiped the tears from her face, placed a sweet kiss on her mother's forehead and leaned toward Lila's ear. "Don't you give up. I'll be back soon."

With one last look, Sasha joined Judah in the hallway. His body was tense, and his gaze bounced between the stairwell door and the elevators. She'd never seen him so anxious. "Okay, I'm ready."

He placed a hand on her upper back and guided her toward the elevators. They hadn't gone but a few steps when blue lights flashed around them. Sasha turned back to the source of the strobe. The light was located above her mother's door.

Loud bells dinged around them, and several staff members rushed past. Sasha flattened herself against the wall to let them by and then fell into step behind them. She had to make sure her mother was okay. The doctor had just told her she was going to make a full recovery. Surely she hadn't coded as soon as Sasha had stepped from the room.

"Sasha, wait."

She didn't slow down for Judah. She had to get to her mom. A team of health-care professionals wheeled a red cart into her mother's room, and she stood in the hallway keeping out of their way. One nurse performed chest compressions. The other pulled medicines and more IV bags from the drawers. A different doctor rushed in and gave orders. Loud alarms and beeps from the display continued to blare in her ears.

"She's still in V-fib." The nurse in blue scrubs pressed a couple of buttons on the defibrillator.

The doctor moved to the foot of the bed and pulled on gloves. "Let's shock her at two hundred, please."

Judah's hand pressed against her shoulder. "We have to go."

"I can't. I have to see."

"Continue CPR and let's drop one mg of epinephrine."

The doctor clasped his hands behind his back while the nurse inserted a needle into the line. "One mg of epi given."

"Good. Let me know when two minutes has passed."

Another nurse stepped in to do chest compressions for a while, but her mother's rhythm remained chaotic. "Dr. Hall. Two minutes."

"Shock again at three hundred."

Everyone stepped back from her mother's bed, and another jolt was sent into her body.

"We have systole and a normal rhythm. She's no longer in V-fib. Continue to monitor her and alert me to any changes." The doctor removed his gloves and stepped from the room.

The normal cadence of her mother's heart monitor was music to Sasha's ears. Judah slipped his arm around her shoulders, and she turned in to his chest, a release of her tears wetting his shirt.

The elevator doors at the end of the hall dinged open. Sasha looked up. Three tattooed men stepped off and moved in their direction. Judah pushed her toward the stairwell door at the opposite end of the corridor. NX5 members wouldn't let a code blue stop them from killing her on sight.

Judah took the stairs two at a time toward the roof with Sasha headed up in front of him. He wasn't sure if the gang members had noticed their presence with all the activity in the hallway. He prayed the commotion would camouflage their movement until they could escape, but he couldn't take any chances. "Hurry."

A metal door clanged below, and heavy footsteps echoed in the vertical corridor. He looked over the railing and spotted tattooed men several flights down. He and Sasha had a good head start, but it wouldn't take these guys long to catch up with their muscular legs and bulging biceps. He just hoped their cardio was lacking. He and Sasha needed to put as much distance between them and the gang members as possible.

The stagnant air in the stairwell made breathing a challenge, but Judah didn't slow down. The muscles in his legs burned something awful, and he figured Sasha was exhausted from overexertion, too, but she kept going. "How far up?"

"Three more flights."

Sasha picked up the pace, pulled open the door when they reached the top floor and Judah stepped into another hallway behind her. The space was quiet, and in front of them two large doors opened into a large room with a stage situated down front. Rows of chairs filled the rest of the area, and a large conference table sat at the back. Judah moved toward a pair of sliding doors opposite the auditorium that opened onto the roof.

Sasha followed and moved to the edge. "What now? There's no way down."

Blades from a helicopter chopped the air above them as it disappeared on the other side of the building. They ran around the corner and spotted emergency crews unloading a stretcher to wheel a patient inside.

Judah approached the pilot, who still sat inside the fuselage. He held up his badge and motioned for the man to open his door.

"We need you to take us to the police precinct."

The pilot shook his head. "I can't do that. It's against hospital policy."

"I'll make sure to clear you with the hospital if you just give us a lift. It's police business."

The pilot stared at his badge. "Let me clear it with my super—"

Gunfire erupted from the far end of the building. The man's eyes widened. "Get in."

Judah returned fire for cover while Sasha ran around the front of the helicopter and climbed in the back. He moved toward the passenger side. More bullets chased his feet. The chopper might be a death trap, but it was their only means of escape—and only if the pilot lifted off within seconds.

One man exited out a different side door of the hospital across from Judah's window and raised a gun. "Get down."

Three officers tackled the assassin before he could get a shot off.

The pilot swept the chopper from the side of the building and lifted the craft into the air, escaping another barrage of gunfire from the first three. Judah cranked his neck and looked back to the roof. The SWAT unit had moved in and surrounded all four suspects, who surrendered and were handcuffed.

Judah would have his chance to interview each one after they were processed. If he could get them to turn on Coby Evans, maybe he could end the man's plan to take out Sasha and finally put Hank's killer behind bars.

"Where did you say you needed to go?" The pilot maneuvered the cyclic and steered the craft toward the edge of town.

"The police precinct." Judah looked over at him. "Where'd you learn to fly like that?"

"Afghanistan. I learned a few maneuvers and defensive tactics from flying a medical helicopter in a war zone."

"That was more than a few. Must've been difficult."

"Most things worth doing are difficult. We saved hundreds of soldiers' lives and even some of our Afghan allies."

"I bet you've got some stories to tell."

"I do. God did some amazing things during my time there. The only reason I'm here today to help you is because of Him."

"I'm sure your skills had something to do with it, too." Judah rested his head back and released the breath he'd been holding. "Seems like people would have enough respect for the injured to leave a medical helicopter alone, no matter where you are located. I guess that's not the case in a war zone."

"Our enemies had no problem taking out military hospitals or medical helicopters. They figured the more of us they killed, the better. A pilot learns real quick how to avoid getting shot down—sometimes the aviation books just don't teach what real-world experience does."

"Thanks for helping us just now. We really appreciate it," Sasha said through her headset. "I'm not sure what we would've done had you not been here."

"Just because we escaped doesn't mean they won't follow you. A helicopter's kind of hard to hide. If they have runners on the ground, which I'm sure they do, they'll follow us to the precinct. What did you do to warrant all the attention?"

"I'm an eyewitness in a murder, and the killer wants me dead so I can't testify against him."

"If she does, he'll go away for life, and gang members don't take to kindly to that." Judah looked down at the roads beneath them. "At least we'll have backup at the precinct. I'm texting Sergeant Quinn to make sure he's ready for us."

The pilot steered the craft over the tops of trees and flew the few miles to the precinct, then set the helicopter down in the police department parking lot. Judah helped Sasha exit, thanked the pilot and rushed her inside the building without incident.

He moved through the familiar hallways and toward the bullpen. They needed to share the latest incident and write up a report, but when he passed by the conference room, he saw Leila sitting at the table with a dark-haired man and a woman who seemed familiar. DA Alex Strut's voice echoed through a phone in the middle of the table. The couple sat with their back to the door and held hands. Judah couldn't make out who they were from this angle. He slowed his steps.

"Looks like DA Strut didn't make it in person. Maybe we can interrupt his call so you can tell him the man who attacked you wasn't the coffee shop owner."

"Sounds good."

He stepped inside the conference room, and Sasha followed. The unidentified man and woman turned toward them.

Judah stopped in his tracks, pulled his weapon and aimed it at Coby Evans. The woman rolled her chair back and raised her hands, but Coby sat there, unmoving, with a smug smile on his face.

"Put your hands on your head."

"Wait, Judah." Leila held up a hand as she stood from her chair. "They're helping us."

"He's Hank's murderer and just sent assassins to attack us at the hospital. He's *not* here to help us."

"Now, Detective, I'd have to be one brave man to walk into a police precinct and assassinate a woman." Coby looked over his shoulder at his girlfriend, then straightened, placed his palms on the back of his head and shifted his cold black stare to Sasha.

EIGHT

Judah cuffed Coby and escorted him to the holding cell, then slammed the door closed, giving a strong jerk on the bars to make sure the lock held. If he had his way, this would be Coby's view for the rest of his life—on the inside looking out.

"You know I'm innocent." Coby's tone was calm, as if he knew his current position was temporary.

Heat rushed through every fiber of Judah's body, and if they'd been in an open room together, he wasn't sure what he might've done. Good thing the bars were between them. "Tell someone who believes you."

He turned to go, not wanting to lose his cool and incur some kind of disciplinary action.

"It's true."

Judah stopped and faced him again. "We both know you killed Hank, and I'm going to find enough evidence so you spend the rest of your life in jail."

"Problem is the evidence will exonerate me, and as an upstanding officer, I'm sure you want to be certain to put the right person behind bars."

"We've got the right person. All I need to figure out is how your girlfriend helped you."

A flash of darkness crossed his face. Judah had hit a

nerve. "She doesn't have anything to do with this. I want protection for her. That's why we're here."

"If she doesn't have anything to do with Hank's murder, then why does she need protection?"

"Because I have enemies, and they will do whatever they can to make me suffer."

If he was using the woman to gain sympathy, then his strategy wouldn't work, but there was genuine concern in his tone. Judah decided to bite in order to gain more information. "And who does she need protection from?"

"Soberano."

Judah stared at him for a moment. "Now you're just wasting my time."

"It means 'the sovereign.' That's the kingpin who runs NX5."

"And you know who Soberano is?"

"I do, and they'll keep coming for Monica and me unless we have protection."

Judah stepped back and leaned against the wall. He'd never heard of Soberano before, despite all his years working homicide. Most of the murders in Shadow Creek fell into one or two areas, domestic violence or gang-related crime, but Soberano was not a name that ever came up. "And who is Monica to you?"

"Have you ever loved someone so much you'd be willing to do anything for them?"

Judah thought of Sasha, but the less Coby knew about his private life, the better. He didn't want to bond with this criminal over unrequited love. This was a time to get a confession regarding his best friend's murder. "Is that why you killed Hank? For her?"

The man hesitated, and a small smile curled the corners of his lips. "I have information that could save Sasha

Kane's life, but if you continue to obsess over accusing me, then she'll never be safe. Not as long as Soberano's handing out the orders."

Judah pressed up from the wall and crossed to the bars. "This isn't a game. Making up names to throw the heat off you is not going to work, so you need to come clean. You were there and you killed Hank. What I want to know is why."

"I was there but I didn't kill him. Soberano did."

"You saw him?"

"Caught a glimpse of him when the gun fired, and I'd know his voice anywhere. He was the one arguing with Hank before I found your friend dead."

"Then why don't you give him up instead of keeping his secret? If you were there and you saw him pull the trigger, we can put him behind bars instead of you. You need to be willing to give him up."

"I'm not exactly innocent, Detective. Hank was helping me, and without him working my case, I'll go to prison. The man had a legal mind like I've never seen. Without him, I'll be convicted and sent to the state penitentiary, I'll be dead before the guards ring the first dinner bell. I need immunity and protection, which is the reason I've been trying to work out a deal with your officers. And the reason I've kept Soberano's identity to myself. That's the only leverage I've got."

Judah paced the floor in front of the cell. The more Coby talked, the more sense he made, even though his reluctance to name names frustrated Judah. He was right. If he went to jail, his enemies would shank him in no time. He'd be a sitting duck inside a cell, and even though Judah wasn't completely convinced Coby didn't have something to do with Hank's death, he couldn't ignore the fact that he'd be sending the man to his certain death. "Then why not just disappear and keep your secret?"

"Soberano has a global reach and—he is trying to merge several cartels underneath his command. If he does that, then he'll have the largest trafficking network in this part of the world. Only the US marshals have a strong enough reputation to keep me protected from someone like that."

Judah took a step closer. "Fine. I'll talk to Leila, but you'll have to give up his identity. We can't provide tax-payer-funded protection and get nothing in return."

"Once I'm cleared for all my other indiscretions and have immunity in writing, I'll give you the identity. I can't go to prison, Detective. You must understand that."

"I understand the truth."

"And I'm speaking the truth." Coby shifted his weight and pushed his hands into the pockets of his jeans. "Like I said before, I'm not the one who killed Hank, or anyone else, for that matter."

"You attacked Officer Kane and tried to run over her with an SUV. That's attempted murder on law enforcement. Enough to keep you behind bars for a long time."

"I wasn't going to kill her. I just needed to scare her into silence and take the camera."

"So you admit to being at Hank's murder scene."

"True, I was there, but that doesn't mean I took his life. I didn't even have a gun on me. I might be a drug dealer, but I'm not a murderer." The man took a seat on the hard bench bolted to the wall. "You've got the wrong guy."

"We'll see about that." Judah walked away again, then turned back. "If you're lying, which wouldn't be a shock, you're looking at life without parole. I won't let them give you anything less."

"That's a long sentence for felony distribution and drug

trafficking. That's what Hank was working on for me when I walked into the office that day. Soberano was yelling at him over losing some case. I started to intervene, but then a fight broke out and Soberano shot him. I didn't want him to see me or I'd be a dead man, too. So I hid. After he left, I went to check on Hank, but it was too late. Sasha came in and I went back to my hiding place inside the closet. I figured if she found me, she'd arrest me, and then I'd go to prison for a crime I didn't commit. I had to get out of there, but then she called the police and started taking photos."

"And that's when you assaulted her and tried to strangle her. You're far from innocent. We have multiple charges to prove your guilt and add to your rap sheet."

"She took photos of my face. I wasn't going to kill her. I just wanted the SD card so she wouldn't have a picture of me. Doesn't matter now. The DA has agreed to put me in WITSEC in exchange for my testimony. You have no control over what they offer me."

Judah would have to have a talk with DA Strut. His history was to go soft on criminals, but he'd make sure to see justice in Hank's case. "I won't let you lie your way into a lesser charge. I'll make sure he knows the truth about you."

"Doesn't really matter if you believe me or not. I'm the only one who knows the identity of Hank's killer and the person who wants Sasha dead. When DA Strut provides immunity, then you'll be able to keep the woman you love safe. Plus, I'll tell you how the entire operation works and you can bring the whole network down."

"So you can take over where Soberano left off?"

"I don't need that kind of stress. The man is paranoid. Thinks everyone's out to kill him. I don't want to live like that."

Judah wasn't about to fall for Coby's games, but one

thing was still nagging him. "Did Hank work for Soberano, too?"

"Not directly, but Hank provided a defense for one of Soberano's allies."

"And won?"

"Unfortunately, no."

Hank had only lost one case recently, unless there was another defeat hidden away in his friend's office files. "Was that your brother's case?"

"Someone else's. Not sure who exactly. He did a good job of keeping the details out of the papers, and honestly at that time I was out of town on another assignment for Soberano. Wasn't really on my radar since the charges didn't include me."

With Nelson and Leila working Hank's case, Judah hadn't looked through his friend's case files. He'd reach out to them both and see if they had any information to back up Coby's claims. If the man was telling the truth, then maybe they could use that info to uncover Soberano's identity and deny Coby immunity. Why let one criminal off just to get another? This way they could put them both away.

Judah walked toward the hall door.

"It would be best if you supported my immunity with DA Strut," Coby said, moving back to the bars. "I have valuable information if you want to keep Sasha and your son safe."

Judah clasped the cold metal door handle and paused at the man's last words. Coby Evans knew he had a son. That meant Soberano knew, too.

Sasha and Bodie were the most important people in his life now, but if he helped Coby with immunity, Judah might never get justice for Hank. He had to figure out a way to keep them safe *and* put Coby behind bars.

Judah made his way to the evidence room and completed the check-in process, then scoured the shelves for several boxes of Hank's case files. He shifted through many of the items the investigators collected at the scene, but the last box he opened held hundreds of folders all labeled with every defendant's name. Judah pulled the box from the shelf, found a long table against the wall and examined the folder's contents looking for any client who was an obscure associate of NX5.

An hour passed, and still he hadn't found a connection between Hank and the case. Instead of wasting more time, he took photos of the remaining documents and returned everything to the shelves before heading back to the conference room.

"Where have you been?" Sasha leaned toward him when he took his seat.

"Had some reports to look over."

"Glad you could join us again, Detective. I've just received approval from the judge to enter Coby and Monica into WITSEC. We've decided to give him immunity in exchange for his testimony." The rustle of papers sounded on DA Strut's end of the line. "Or I can charge him with felony drug trafficking and distribution and send him to prison, where he'll remain in protective custody until we arrest this Soberano he keeps saying is the head of NX5."

"Prison gets my vote." Judah leaned back in his chair. "I'm not convinced he's being truthful. In all the years I've worked for the gang unit, I've never heard of Soberano. Coby's a known liar and criminal. Who's to say he's not making up this person to save his own skin and throw us off our case by telling us someone else killed Hank? He had means, motive and opportunity. We've put other homicidal maniacs away with a lot less."

Leila leaned forward. "I have to disagree with Detective Walker. Even if Evans isn't being truthful, we can't take any chances of losing this guy until we have more evidence. I know he's not an innocent man by any means, but I also don't want to put him away thinking this case is wrapped up when the real killer is still out there running a dangerous criminal organization."

"And do we have any evidence that proves he's being truthful?" Judah asked. "Because unless we do, this guy deserves hard prison time, if not for murder then for all the drug-trafficking charges against him."

"We *do* have blood evidence that could corroborate his story. The photos from the crime scene show files open on Hank's desk after he was killed, and they were covered in blood. Now, some of this is Hank's, but—" Leila tapped her tablet and motioned to the large smart board on the wall "—CSU found two types of blood on these documents. We ran the samples at the crime lab, and we have a second set of DNA."

"And you think it belongs to the killer?"

"We think so, but we haven't hit a match yet. If it is the killer's DNA, then he might not be in CODIS."

"Hank had plenty of clients who entered and exited his office every day. Could it be one of theirs?"

"Maybe. There is always the chance of cross-contamination, but with it being two different blood types, too, we know there was a second person in the room who fought with Hank and was injured. Plus, Hank didn't have any clients scheduled that day. His receptionist said he cleared his calendar so he could get caught up on his stack of files. And there were no meetings or hearings that we know about other than Sasha's."

Leila tapped a few keys and picked up a laser pointer

from the table. "See here? That's the blood spatter we sampled. With no one scheduled to enter the office, then the only explanation is the evidence belongs to the killer."

"Wait." Sasha held up her hand. "Where did you get these crime scene photos? My camera was stolen and everything I uploaded to the cloud was hacked and erased."

"Judah had them."

All eyes shifted to him. "I downloaded them after you gave me the card. I guess I got them to my hard drive before anyone deleted yours."

Leila continued and scrolled down to another photo. "His receptionist stated no one entered while she was there, and she locked the front door when she left. According to her experience, Hank's not one to open the door if he's buried in work, even if a walk-in knocks."

Judah turned to Sasha. "Did he cancel on you?"

"No. He gave me the code to the back entrance and told me to come in that way instead of through the front."

"Then if he gave that option to you, he might've given the same code to someone else."

Leila pulled up photos of the back staircase. "There weren't any cameras at this entrance. From my understanding, Hank usually kept it locked but it's possible that's how someone entered and bypassed the security cameras."

"I guess he needed an entrance that would provide anonymity for his more questionable clients and members of NX5," Judah said.

Another photo popped up on the screen. Judah leaned forward in his chair. "Can you magnify that one right there?"

Leila clicked on the thumbnail. "Do you see something?"

"Not sure. Can you enlarge this area?" He stood and moved toward the large monitor while Leila magnified the section indicated.

"All I see is a blurry image of Coby at the bottom of the fire escape."

"Here." He pointed to the upper right-hand corner of the image. "There, in the shadows, parked in the corner of the garage. That looks like a woman sitting in the same dark van that almost ran me and Sasha over. Do you recognize her?"

"I don't, and the quality isn't great. Let me send it to tech and see if they can get a better visual."

"I'd like to know if she's just a random bystander, his getaway driver or the woman he brought with him today. Where'd she go anyway?"

"I put her in soft holding. Gave her some coffee, tried to get her to turn on Coby but she holds to his version of the events."

"Make sure we have a good photo of her on security cameras or something. She could've been helping him."

"Agreed. No one mentioned her before." Leila flipped through a couple of screens. "We had officers canvass that area, too, and no one mentioned a woman inside our perimeter." She tried to focus the image as much as her software would allow. "Definitely a job for tech. The image is too pixelated and blurry on my computer. Hopefully they can clean the photo up enough so we can get an ID. Unfortunately, we don't have anything in our gang unit records, past or present, about a woman being a leader in NX5."

"Tell me about the blood spatter again." Even though everything inside Judah screamed of Coby's guilt, he had to let the evidence lead him, not his gut.

"We think Hank was working on the papers, the attacker enters, they struggled with Hank, who got at least a few good punches in and caused the second set of blood spatter before he died." Leila riffled through some of the papers in her folder and slid one across the table to him. "The lab report stated the pattern was different on the documents than the wall, and the blood type tests didn't match Hank or Coby."

"Run them through CODIS again and see if there are any female matches. If she's in the DNA database, then we can bring her in for questioning." Judah raked a hand through his hair.

"Do you really think Hank would fight with a woman?"

"Only if she was planning to kill him. If not, then we're back to a nameless, faceless killer out there who wants Sasha dead and no closer to figuring out their identity."

DA Strut, who'd been listening through the speaker the entire time, sighed. "Wrong. We have Coby, and he can give us a name. I'm not willing to go back to square one on this. If the DNA is inconclusive, I'm offering him a deal."

"What *you* have is an unreliable criminal who is desperate to save himself and his girlfriend," Judah said. "We can't trust any name out of his mouth."

"He's all we've got." Leila snapped her laptop lid closed. "Whether we can trust him or not, he's the only piece in this network we have."

"Let's keep working. With the three of us, we can figure out a solution that doesn't let this guy off easy. Hank was my best friend and one of the best defense attorneys in the area. He deserves justice."

"I'll do my best, but sometimes we don't always get what we want, Judah, no matter how hard we work," Strut said. "I'll put together the paperwork so the deal will be ready just in case. Keep me posted if you discover anything else that will help us move in another direction."

A click resonated through the speaker as DA Strut ended his call. Judah struggled with the fact the man was so quick to give Coby a plea deal. The move might be easier, but with the man's pattern of criminal behavior, Judah wanted to investigate further. Make sure they'd done everything possible before handing Coby a get-out-of-jail-free card. At least speaking up had bought the officers a bit more time and Coby was still sitting behind bars—exactly where he belonged. "Where did officers pick up Coby? At his home?"

Leila collected her papers from the table. "At the hospital. Said he was there with Monica."

"At the exact same time Sasha and her mom are there? The SWAT team took down four of Coby's gang members. That can't be a coincidence." Judah took his seat at the table again.

Leila shrugged. "He said she was having some pregnancy complications they wanted to get checked out."

"And we confirmed that with the hospital?"

"I'm still waiting for the hospital to release Monica's health records but was able to get confirmation from one of the ER nurses who cared for her."

"She volunteered that information? I thought they could get fired for violating HIPAA rules."

"They can, but when she found out Coby was a suspect in Hank's murder, she talked, quietly, and begged me not to tell her superiors. She said she wanted to do the right thing since Hank had helped her in a legal matter."

"Seems a bit unethical—and convenient."

"True, but I'll take what we can get."

"Is Monica still pregnant?"

"According to the nurse, she was when she left the hospital, but I'm not sure if something has happened since." Leila flipped through a couple of her sticky notes. "We can ask her during the WITSEC meeting tomorrow morning."

Judah stood again and began to pace. "Why do I feel like we're getting played?"

"That's what happens when your desire to bring down a certain criminal outweighs the evidence," Leila said. "Besides, how do you think Coby's playing us?"

"I'm not sure. I just hope it's not too late when we figure out what he's up to."

"He said he wanted a fresh start for his soon-to-be wife and daughter. That's why he's pushing so hard to stay out of prison. I can imagine having a baby could change a man's direction in life."

Judah looked at Sasha, who met his gaze. He was still processing the fact he was a father and knew his life would never be the same. Maybe the same thing had happened to Coby. "What's the girlfriend's last name again?"

Leila clicked her mouse. "Hernandez."

If this guy was telling the truth and the evidence backed him up, then Judah would have to take his word that someone else had killed Hank and targeted his new family. But until he had the cold, hard proof otherwise in his hands, his mind was set on Coby Evans—and maybe the new girl in his life.

"How did she seem when you brought them in? Nervous? Worried?"

"Calm, actually," Leila said.

"Can we pull up the photo from the van in the garage again?" Judah stepped toward the screen when Leila pulled up the picture. "Do we have a current photo too? Maybe on social media or something?"

"Here's one from her profile."

"Now put them side by side." He smiled. "Sure, looks like the same girl to me, blurry or not."

"How about now?" Leila tapped a couple of more keys. "I just got the adjusted picture back from tech."

"So Monica was at the scene of the crime and was driving the van that almost ran us over. She needs to be questioned."

"I'm on it." Leila retrieved her phone.

Judah turned to Sasha. "You ready to go? I'll take you back to the safe house."

"Almost. Leila, what about Mr. Bell, the coffee shop owner? Is he still being held?" Sasha asked.

Her sister looked through her files. "He was released on bond, but if Coby provides the information we need, then we'll drop all charges against him. Let's just hope he leads us to Hank's real murderer."

"Don't count on it." Judah leaned against the wall.

"I have to," Leila said. "There's too much riding on this, and he doesn't want to end up in jail like his brother."

"Sounds like everything's coming together, tied up with a neat little bow." Sasha stood, and Judah followed her to the door.

"Yeah. A little too neat." Judah made a mental note to talk to Strut about his plan. He wanted to make sure the district attorney didn't dismiss any factual evidence. Alex was known to hand out easy plea deals in an effort to avoid trials and keep his closure rate high. At least Leila was working with him and Nelson. She wanted to keep Sasha safe as much as he did, but even so, something about the entire situation made him uneasy.

They waited in the precinct lounge until one of the patrol officers arrived to take them back to the hospital, where he'd left the car. He didn't want Sasha out in the open in case they were being followed by more of Coby's guys.

The moon lit up the room as Sasha took the seat beside

him and looked out the window. "I guess they'll be easy to spot with a full moon if they come after me again tonight."

"Let's hope they don't."

She faced forward in the seat. "Ever feel like this all seems a little too easy?"

"Yeah, and I don't like it." He stood and walked to the exit door. "Our ride's here. Let's get the car from the hospital and head back to the safe house. I'll feel better once you're in hiding again."

Judah held the door as Sasha stood and adjusted the strap of her bag.

"I keep asking myself why Coby Evans would give himself up. Why not just leave?" she asked. "He has the resources, with his high position in NX5, and after his brother's death, I'm sure he could've pulled some strings to get out of the country or at least lay low for a while."

"Not if Soberano wants him dead. If this person is real, then Coby is the only one who knows his identity, and according to Coby he has a long reach."

"True. Still, seems like Coby would have friends in another country who could help him out and make him disappear."

Maybe she had a point. Coby's move did seem out of character. Not many gang members reached out to the cops unless they had no other choice. "Speaking of lying low—keep your head down as we cross the parking area."

She nodded, jogged to the car and slid into the back seat, leaving the door open for Judah.

He sat beside her. So far so good. No one shot at them or seemed to be following their driver. All was quiet, which made him uneasy. "Gang relations are tricky. If what Coby says is true about this Soberano, then the man could have a network that covers North and South America. If Soberano believes Coby ratted him out, then he'll want Coby dead. WITSEC has a strong record of keeping people safe if they agree to the terms. This might be his best play."

Their driver wound through the streets of Shadow Creek, then pulled into the hospital parking garage. Judah pointed out Chelsea's car to the man, then opened the door for Sasha to exit when he stopped.

"You don't believe his act, do you? You think he's guilty of killing Hank and trying to pin it on Soberano."

"I think he's lying, but I've been wrong before. Your sister's right. We need to follow the evidence, and if what we gather proves Coby's story is true, then I'll be on board to help him disappear. In fact, I'd love to see him gone from Shadow Creek, even though another will step in and take his place before his plane lands. Too bad we can't dismantle the whole organization."

Judah pulled the keys from his pocket and hit the unlock button. Sasha opened her door, but she didn't get inside. "Maybe. I'm not sure what to believe anymore."

"That's why the evidence speaks for itself. Nelson and Leila are working the case. They're some of the best homicide investigators I know. They'll put together a good case and get to the truth."

She leaned against the side of Chelsea's car. "I'm impressed. You've never backed down from your opinions on a case, especially when the victim is someone you know."

"I have faith in our team—and I don't really have any other option. The case is not in my control." Judah twirled the key ring on his finger, which slipped off the end and dropped to the ground. He knelt to pick it up and noticed a red light flashing underneath the car. A timer counted down—ten...nine...

"Sasha, run!"

Judah straightened, bolted for the exit and reached back for Sasha's hand, but an invisible force propelled them apart. Heat singed his skin then subsided. Debris pelted his body and instant ringing concussed through his head. Black smoke veiled his vision and choked the oxygen from his lungs.

With a roll onto his side, he scanned the area around him. Chunks of concrete littered the garage opening, and small pieces of gravel continued to rain down over him. He didn't see Sasha and prayed she'd been able to get far enough away from the explosion.

Judah belly-crawled back toward what was left of the vehicle. Pain pierced his body with every move, but he had to get to her.

She moaned from somewhere to his left. He switched direction and pushed to his feet, triggering a piercing throb through his head, then moved toward her voice. Her silhouette was crumpled on the ground in a fetal position three feet from him. He reached her, lifted her limp body into his arms and noted a deep gash on her forehead. He had to get her to the emergency room before NX5 returned to complete the job.

A loud knocking noise roused Sasha awake. She opened her eyes to a dim light filtering through a large hole at her feet and tried to sit up, but the confines of the restrictive space limited her mobility. She was inside a tube—most likely an MRI machine—but nothing made sense as to why she was there. Her fuzzy memory only intensified as the loud knocking noise thumped rhythmically with the pain in her head.

She closed her eyes again, unable to fight the heaviness of her eyelids. Muffled voices echoed into the room while everything else moved in slow motion. She inhaled and the scent of bleach burned her nose. This had to be some kind of hospital room, but who'd brought her here and how long had she been there? Her tongue stuck to the roof of her mouth when she tried to ask for a cup of water.

An intercom buzzed. "Ms. Kane. Please hold still. We're almost finished getting our images."

The man's deep voice soothed her for the moment, but unanswered questions plagued her mind. MRI images? Maybe the pain in her head was something serious. She stilled like she'd been told. She'd need a good study to find out what was wrong with her, but if they didn't get her out of this medical coffin soon, a full-on panic attack would ensue.

After several more excruciating minutes, the table slid forward and a technologist helped her back onto her stretcher, then wheeled her into the transport area.

Judah stood leaning against a wall and straightened when she exited. "You're awake."

"And feel like I've been run over by a truck. What happened?"

His eyes widened. "You don't remember?"

"Only the car service picking us up at the precinct. What am I doing in the hospital? I remember that we were headed back here to get Chelsea's car, but I don't remember anything once we arrived."

"There was an explosion. Someone planted a bomb under Chelsea's car. We barely escaped before the device went off. I happened to see the timer and was able to get a little farther away, but you were closer and have some injuries from the force and shrapnel."

"Well, I'm glad you were able to escape any serious injuries. In fact, you don't look like you have a scratch on you."

Judah nodded at the technologist, who locked the stretcher in place and left them to wait for transport. "I got checked out, don't worry."

"What did they find?"

Judah pointed toward a large, burly man, mid-thirties with tattoos and dressed in scrubs, who entered the area. "Looks like your ride is here."

She ignored the obvious swerve from her question but made a mental note to bring it up again when she got back to the ER. Judah seemed tense, and he was keeping something from her. Instead of peppering him with questions, she kept quiet while he walked beside the stretcher. She was thankful he didn't leave her unguarded for a minute.

Their transport person wheeled her to the patient elevator and pressed the key. Judah stepped up beside her. "Are you in any pain right now?"

"My head feels like it's been run over by a Mack truck, but other than a few sore muscles, I'm okay. I'll take some ibuprofen when I get back to the room. I can't believe you don't have more injuries, too—after all, it's not every day a person survives an explosion."

The transport tech pulled her stretcher into the elevator when the doors opened, and they rode up the third floor before the doors opened again and he pushed her forward. Sasha held up a hand. "Excuse me. Isn't the ER on the second floor? We need to go down one more level." Sasha pointed to the other hallway.

"You're in room D352, correct?" the man asked.

Judah took her hand. "The ER doctors admitted you to the hospital, Sasha." He nodded to the transport. "You have the right room."

"That was fast. Usually, a patient remains in the ER

for hours. I was hoping they'd let me go home instead of admitting me."

Judah smiled but still didn't comment. He seemed edgier than normal. Like he wanted to tell her something but wasn't sure how.

The transport tech wheeled her down the hallway and into a room with a view of the mountains. Blue skies stretched in the distance, and the sun beamed through the window. Three of her sisters stood when the man wheeled her past two armed officers and then helped her back into her bed before leaving.

Leila smothered her with a relieved hug once she was settled under the covers, while Holly fluffed her pillows and Dani straightened the blanket.

Leila took a seat on the edge of her bed, clasping her hand. "Thank goodness you're okay. We were so worried. Are you in any pain?"

"Just a headache. Anybody got ibuprofen?"

Dani hit a button on a remote. "I'll tell the nurse to bring you some."

"Okay. What aren't you telling me?" Sasha asked and made contact with each of her sisters. They'd never been so attentive before. Even when she broke her leg as a child they signed her cast and moved on to more interesting games while she was stuck inside.

Sasha found Judah's gaze on her from the corner, where he was staying out of the way. She searched his face for any concern about her sisters' weird behavior. He smiled, but the gesture didn't reach his eyes. A sign of a forced expression. Something she'd learned during her interrogation classes at the police academy.

Bouquets of flowers, a multitude of cards and one stuffed teddy bear decorated the windowsill beside him, and more questions came to mind. All these events weren't adding up, and a rush of panic assaulted every nerve in her body. "Where's Chelsea and Bodie?"

Hesitant glances bounced between the women and passed to Judah, who crossed to the other side of the bed and took her fingers in his hand. "First, let me say that Bodie is fine."

"Are you sure? Because y'all are acting weird, and if something has happened to him I want to know. Did NX5 get to him?"

"Not exactly. Chelsea had to take Bodie into Witness Protection. Their location is top secret, and only her superiors know where they are located."

Sasha's breaths shortened with the news, and every nightmare scenario imaginable whirled through her mind. "Is he okay?"

"He's fine." Judah squeezed her fingers. "Chelsea detected the danger and got him out of the house without anyone seeing them, thanks to your father's secret exit. Bodie is safe, but the Whitmore property has been compromised."

She rested her head back on her pillow and stared at the ceiling. "Actually, that's probably what's best. He'll be safe with her. When can I get out of here to see him?"

"Now that you're awake, hopefully soon," Judah said.

"How did they find us? We were so careful to make sure we weren't followed. Only a handful of people knew where we were."

"We're not sure yet, but somehow they discovered the location and found the cabin. NX5 sent a team of five assassins, but Chelsea and Bodie were long gone by the time they breached the house."

Dani placed a cool cloth on her neck. "Maybe we

shouldn't talk about this right now. You are suffering from a head injury, and stress is not going to help you get better."

"I want to know what happened." Sasha sat up straighter but reached for a nearby basin just in case.

Judah took a seat next to her. "Your father's cameras alerted Chelsea when the gang was about two miles out. She was able to use the secret exit to get Bodie out before they arrived. With his stash of ammunition and the secret exit through the floor, she escaped with Bodie and got him to the marshals' office. Their location is now unknown to all of us, unless we enter WITSEC with him."

"But I'm his mother. They'll tell me, right?" She squeezed Judah's fingers.

"Only if you decide to join them."

Sasha pulled her hand away. She wanted to be angry at Chelsea for taking her son away without discussing the important decision with her. They should've waited for her to wake up, but in the end Bodie's safety was all that really mattered. "So Coby was right. Someone *is* still out there pulling the strings. Leila, is there still no word on Soberano's identity? I thought Coby was going to give the name up."

"DA Strut released Coby with the understanding that he would appear for his WITSEC meeting. That's where we planned to have the immunity papers to sign and he would divulge the information, but instead of showing up, he disappeared. He never entered Witness Protection. We aren't sure if Soberano had him killed or if he went off the grid. We called in the FBI to help us look internationally for him."

The news made Sasha want to curl up in a fetal position and cry, but if she was ever going to see Bodie again without having to disconnect from everyone else she'd ever loved, then she had to be strong. "How's Mom?"

Dani stepped forward from where she'd been standing. "She's home and doing well."

Sasha pushed herself up farther in the bed. "But I just saw her a few hours ago and she was intubated. How can she already be home?"

Another hesitant look passed between her sisters and Judah. Their secrecy annoyed her.

"Would y'all stop sharing weird looks and talk to me? And don't sugarcoat it. I have to know what's going on."

Leila took her hand. "It's been more than a few hours since you saw Mom."

At her sister's words, Sasha looked around her room. Flowers, some wilted and some alive, sat in the corner, along with balloons and a get-well card with all of her sisters names on the inside. Some of her T-shirts hung in the wardrobe, and blankets and pillows were stacked on one end of a couch. "How long have I been here?"

Judah ran his thumb across her knuckles. "Five days. You've been in a coma."

Her heart twisted in her chest, and a flood of tears filled her eyes. "I've been away from Bodie that long?"

"He's safe, I promise. Chelsea's been with him the entire time. After the explosion, you didn't wake up, and I gave them permission to take him."

"*You* gave them permission?"

"With you unresponsive, I'm his father and next of kin. I did what I thought was best for our son, to keep him safe."

The thought of Bodie being hidden somewhere in the world without her continued to weaken her resolve. She didn't even know where he was located. She pulled her hand from Judah's and swiped her wet cheeks, then pulled back the covers. "Take me to him. I want to see him."

Judah stood to block her exit from the bed. "You have to be discharged first. We don't know his location, either. Chelsea has him under strict guard."

"Then put me in WITSEC. I'm not spending one more day without him." She moved her legs over the edge of the bed and sat up. Her head swirled, and she swayed forward.

Judah caught her. "You need to rest and the doctor will have to check you out before we can go anywhere. You've been in a coma and your body needs to recuperate."

Leila stepped up and rested a hand on her shoulder. "I'll go get the doctor so he can check you out. If he releases you, then and only then will we go to the marshals' office. They'll want you to enter the program since we still haven't caught Hank's killer, but remember, if you enter WITSEC, you have to leave everything else behind."

Pain ached behind her eyes, and her vision blurred as more tears slipped down her cheeks. "I have to see my son. Can't we set up a visit? I'll follow all the rules, but I have to see him."

Judah helped her recline back into bed. "We'll figure out a way. I'd like to see him, too. Now that you're awake, we'll talk with Chelsea and see what can be arranged, but with Soberano still wanting you dead, we'll need a secure place."

"What about the property we bought?"

"The acre with the barn? Where we planned to get married before…"

His words trailed off as if the memories of their botched relationship were too painful to discuss. "Yes. We can stay in the barn, since the interior has been remodeled. The location is secluded, and we could set up a strong presence of guards around the perimeter."

"After what happened at Whitmore—" Leila said "—a property that wasn't vetted by the marshals' office, I'm not sure they'll approve another unofficial location. Let me contact their office and see if they have an approved place for us to meet. They're experts at keeping witnesses safe, and I think we should go where they suggest. I can't risk Soberano finding you again."

"Who is Soberano again?" Sasha rolled her eyes when he and her sisters shared another look. "I'm sure my memory will come back, but for now can you fill me in?"

Leila grabbed a marker and wrote the name on the medical whiteboard. "The name means 'sovereign.' He's the new kingpin running NX5. Apparently, there was a turf war and he emerged from the shadows, but he has a network set up to keep his identity a secret. Coby was his right-hand man and did all his dirty work, but when he and Monica disappeared, we never learned Soberano's true identity."

Judah folded his arms across his chest. "We should've put more pressure on him to talk when we had him locked up, but Coby refused to tell us anything until he had his immunity docs in front of him. DA Strut let him go with the agreement Coby would show up for his WITSEC meeting, provide them with the name and sign all his immunity documents. When he didn't show, we lost our chance."

"Why would he not show up? That was the only chance for him to survive outside NX5." Sasha took a sip of water.

"We think NX5 took them out," Leila said.

"I'm not so sure about that." Judah took Sasha's cup and replaced it on the side table. "Their bodies would've surfaced by now as a warning for others not to cross Soberano."

Sasha rested her head back against her pillow. She really didn't care about any kingpin or missing gang member. A near-death experience had a way of refocusing what was important, and the only thing that mattered to her was holding Bodie in her arms again. "Just get me to my son."

NINE

After the doctor signed the discharge papers, Judah organized a heavily guarded transport to a new safe house set up through the US marshals' office. The nondescript gray van provided safe passage for the hour-long drive without any tails. Chelsea had agreed that one county over from Shadow Creek was the minimum distance she could approve to keep Bodie safe during their supervised meeting.

They pulled into the quaint town of Waynesville, North Carolina, just after midnight. Most of the local shops and restaurants here were closed by 9:00 p.m. The quiet atmosphere made this the perfect place to hide Sasha and Bodie. Any activity outside the few taverns in the area would raise red flags and spotlight any nefarious plans NX5 and Soberano might have. He prayed they didn't find them.

Sasha unbuckled her seat belt and faced him. "Do you have my phone? I need to text my mom and tell her I love her. The last time I saw her, she was sedated."

"We trashed your old phone. We couldn't take the chance it was hacked. I'm sure we can work out getting a message to her, though. She's doing well with her physical therapy."

Sasha smiled. "She never was one to stay down for long. She learned that Kane toughness from my father and knows how to protect her family."

"That she does." Judah checked his weapon, unwilling to take any chances. If someone did happen to follow them, he'd be ready.

No one was going to hurt Sasha or Bodie as long as he was around. "Listen, I know this probably isn't the best time to bring this up, but the way things have gone since you returned have been chaotic, and we haven't really had a good time to discuss Bodie. Or, to be more specific, my involvement in his life. I know it's going to be complicated, but—"

"It doesn't have to be. I want you in Bodie's life, too. He needs his father, but are you ready for all this? Raising a child isn't easy."

Her question stung. "You don't think I'm responsible enough?"

"That's not what I said. I just want to make sure—"

"I know I haven't had the best parenting examples in my life, but this is different. I deserve a chance to be a good dad. I haven't been able to focus on anything else since I found out, and I've already lost so much time. I'm not going to lose any more."

"Bodie's already in WITSEC, and I'll have to enter, too, if we don't stop NX5. Are you going into the program with us?"

Judah met her gaze. "If you'll have me."

He took her hand in his, but Sasha pulled away. "This isn't about us, Judah. This is about you being a good father to Bodie."

He straightened in his seat. "Of course. I just thought we might be able to pick up where we left off—"

"My first priority is providing as normal a life as possible for our son. I'm not ready for anything romantic with you or anyone else right now."

Her words stung. He'd hoped they could find their way back to each other, but her statement was clear. "Is that something you think might change with time?"

"I don't know."

He'd never expected to be rejected by Sasha a second time, especially when they had a son together.

She tucked a strand of dark hair behind her ear. "I'm sure we can work out some kind of arrangement, maybe the same neighborhood or something." Her tone was cool, matter-of-fact and a bit frustrating.

"I want more. I want my family."

Maybe if he put all his feelings on the table between them, they could find a way to move forward and leave their past behind.

She hesitated, fiddling with a string on her shirtsleeve. "I want more, too, but I can't go back to the way things were."

"But I've been sober for a year now. I'm never going back to that lifestyle."

"And I'm so thankful you're well. It's just that I need a man who puts God first in his life." Her tone was serious.

Why did life's choices always bring him back to God? He'd tried religion before, and nothing had panned out for him. This shouldn't be what keeps them apart.

She continued. "Bodie changed me, in more ways than one."

"I'm sure he did. You're a mom now. That changes everyone."

"Not just that." She raised her gaze to his. "I gave my life to Jesus. I'm not the same woman I used to be, and my faith is important to me. In fact, it's the most important thing to me, and I won't be with someone who doesn't share that."

Judah had noticed a stronger resolve in Sasha since she'd come back, a strength that carried her through even the worst of times and highly stressful situations. He'd always backed away from religion, especially after his mother passed away. He'd cried out to God so many times to save her, but those prayers went unanswered. She was the only person in his life who'd cared about him, and he'd lost her far too soon.

"So, you're saying that we can't be together unless I'm a Christian?"

"I don't mean for it to sound harsh, but yeah. I guess that's what I'm saying."

He faced forward and stared at the closed bookstore in front of him. Several Bibles sat in the window. "And what if I don't buy in to your new faith? Are you going to keep Bodie from me?"

"Of course not. I would never use God to punish you or keep you from our son. That's not His way or mine. I want you to be a part of Bodie's life."

"Even if I don't believe."

"I pray you will someday, but not because of me or Bodie. I want you to believe because you understand God's forgiveness for you."

His heart raced. He'd heard the childhood Bible stories back in the day, but he'd figured either God didn't love him or He didn't exist. So many prayers he'd prayed had gone unanswered, but the light in her eyes and the joy on her face now made him question every dismissal of God he'd made.

Judah shifted in his seat again. "I'm not sure I can do that."

Sasha reached over and placed her hand on top of his.

"That's okay. You don't have to decide right now, but at least give Him some thought. For your own soul."

He held her gaze for a moment, then pulled his hand from hers and exited the vehicle. Enough change had happened in his life over the last week—he wasn't ready for more.

Sasha stepped from the van into the safe house's garage and moved toward the interior door. Her sister had chosen this place to meet since there was little NX5 activity reported here. Their location was a few blocks from the main street and within walking distance of the local precinct. One police guard remained parked outside the garage with two others posted near the entrances of the home. Secure keypad locks and top-of-the-line cameras rounded out the security system.

Small footsteps padded across the hardwood floors when Judah opened the inside door for her. Dark curls bounced on top of Bodie's head as he toddled toward her with arms open wide. "Momma!"

She scooped him up and buried her face into his neck, breathing in the baby-shampoo scent of his hair. "I missed you so much."

He giggled when she smothered him in kisses, then held up the toy in his hand. "Tuck."

She swiped at the wheel giving it a spin. "A blue truck."

Judah emerged from the primary bedroom, where he'd put her bag, and tousled Bodie's curls. "Hey, buddy. That's a cool truck you have there."

Her son held it out for a closer look. "It boo."

"That's a great color. Do you have any more?"

Bodie wiggled to the ground, grabbed Judah's finger and

pulled him toward a rug in the open living area. Chelsea rose from one of the armchairs and joined her with a hug.

"I'm so sorry we had to do things this way. I wanted to talk to you before making the decision, but everything happened so fast. Judah was great. Once he was cleared in the ER, he took action to keep Bodie safe."

"I'm grateful he was there to help with the decision. You did what needed to be done. Thank you."

"Of course. That's my job."

"How did they find the Whitmore property? Dad made sure to keep that off-grid for a reason. Only our family knows about it."

"Not sure yet. But NX5 seems to have resources everywhere. I've got a team looking into it, but there's no connection yet."

Bodie laughed at a silly face Judah made at him. She was thankful they were getting this chance to bond but worried—if she had to enter WITSEC for good and Judah decided not to go, how would that decision hurt Bodie? "How's Bodie doing with everything? With us not being here?"

Chelsea looped an arm through hers and escorted her to the couch. "He's had his moments when he asks for you, but I keep telling him you're coming soon. He thinks we're playing a game and he had to do exactly as I said if he wanted to win. He's been a little trouper."

"No lingering traumatic effects from the attack? I don't want him to be having nightmares about gunmen and running for our lives. He deserves to feel safe and protected."

"Holly assessed him after I set up a covert meeting with her. She said he's doing well, although he did wake up one night with a bad dream and screamed for you. I kept telling him you'd be here soon."

Sasha fought back tears. "I never should've left him."

"You wanted to see Mom—you shouldn't feel guilty about that. We weren't sure what was going to happen with her. Besides, there's no going back. How are you feeling? You had us all worried. I kept tabs on you through Leila."

"I'm good. I don't really remember the explosion, but it seems like everything else is intact."

"I'm glad you still have that brain of yours. We've got to find Soberano before he finds us again so you can come home."

"Are we able to stay here tonight? I know you have been keeping Bodie at another safe house, and I don't want to do anything to put his safety in jeopardy, but I'd love to have one uneventful evening for Judah, Bodie and me to be together. We need this time with him."

Her sister blinked with hesitation. "I thought you were entering the program, too?"

"I am. I'm not leaving him again, but Judah isn't. I want to give them a few more hours."

"Why doesn't he want to enter?"

"He wants to help find Hank's killer first, but I'd like for them to have some more time together before Bodie and I have to disappear."

"Of course. Your new identification documents won't be here until the morning anyway, and there's plenty of room for him to stay one night. We'll transport you and Bodie out first thing in the morning."

"Come on, Momma." Bodie motioned her over with his small hand, and she took a seat on the floor beside Judah. Two years ago, she'd never dreamed she'd be sitting here, on the floor with the love of her life on one side and Bodie on the other, running toy cars around a make-believe track.

Her heart filled with gratitude. *Dear God, please let us have more nights like this—without the danger.*

After an hour, Bodie stretched out on the floor and laid his head on her leg, his eyes bleary with sleep. "I need to put him to bed."

Judah lifted their son into his arms. "Let me."

"How about we both go?"

There was a toddler bed in her room, and Sasha checked all the locks on the windows to make sure they were secure. No one was taking her son that way ever again. Judah placed him in his bed and handed him his blanket before kissing Bodie's forehead. She did the same.

They both stood in the dark room watching their son sleep. Judah slipped his fingers into her hand. "He's amazing."

"That he is."

"I never realized…"

His voice cracked, and she faced him. Judah pulled her into a hug, holding her there. The scent of his muted spice cologne lingered on his shirt. She inhaled and relaxed into his embrace. How she missed moments like this. The intimate security of his warm body next to hers. His breath brushed against her ear. "Thank you."

She pulled back to meet his gaze. "For what?"

"You could've lived in Raleigh forever and I never would've known about him. You gave me a chance even though my past addictions drove us apart. I'm so sorry for putting you through all the drunken, angry tirades that broke us. I don't blame you for not telling me about Bodie back then. You're a good mom and now, because you came back to town, I get to be a father." He kissed her with a gentleness that sent chills to her toes.

She loved this man despite all their baggage. "I wasn't perfect, either, back then."

"But you didn't let alcohol control your life and your decisions."

"No, but I had to learn to trust God in some of the most frightening moments of my life. That wasn't easy when I'd been raised to be self-reliant and independent."

"Maybe there's hope for us yet."

Her heart knew their relationship would never work without God at the forefront, and she was leaving for good tomorrow. If he didn't come with them, this would be the last time she saw him.

She pulled back. "We're leaving tomorrow. Are you sure you won't come with us?"

She longed for his answer to be yes, but when Judah stepped back and dropped his arms from her waist, she had her answer.

"I can't. Not yet."

"Then I guess this will be our last night together for a while." She didn't know when she might see him again or if he would decide to fade from their lives forever.

He brushed his fingers against her cheek. "I guess so."

Tears burned at the corners of her eyes, and she couldn't stand here with him in this room with their son sleeping so peacefully behind them knowing they'd never be a true family. Her heart ached. "I can't do this right now. I'm going to see what Chelsea's doing."

Judah turned back toward Bodie. "I'll be there in a minute. I want to spend a little more time with him."

Before Sasha left the room, she looked back at Judah. He walked to his son's bed, knelt down in front of the window and raised his gaze to the heavens above. When he closed his eyes and bowed his head, she pulled the door closed and said her own silent prayer for Judah to work out his own faith with God.

Sasha entered the living area and found Chelsea sitting cross-legged on the couch shuffling a deck of cards. Her sister held them up. "Hearts?"

"Hopefully."

She was still thinking of Judah, but her sister shot her a puzzled look. "What?"

"Never mind." Sasha motioned toward the table. "You want to sit over here?"

Chelsea pulled an ottoman closer. "Nope. I hate sitting on hard chairs. We can put the cards on this."

"Sounds good to me. I'll shuffle." Sasha held out her hand and looked up when Judah entered the room. His eyes were rimmed red, and he wiped a hand across his face, but his demeanor seemed more at peace. "Can I join you?"

"Of course. We're playing hearts. Do you know it?"

"It's been a while, so remind me."

"The object of the game is to avoid taking hearts or the queen of spades." She snatched the queen of spades during her shuffle and held up the black royalty card. "She comes with a penalty of thirteen points."

Judah took the card from her fingers. "Wait. Say that again."

"There's a penalty of thirteen points?"

"The first part."

"The object of the game is to avoid hearts and the queen of spades."

"Soberano." Judah sat back, still staring at the card. "What did you say the word meant again?"

"'Sovereign.'"

Judah pulled out his phone. "Are you sure the name doesn't end with an *a*? Soberana?"

Sasha followed suit, whipped out her cell and looked it up. The definition for the word was displayed on her screen, and there were two pronunciations. She read them aloud. "'Soberana means sovereign queen. The other is sovereign king.'"

Judah flipped the card between his fingers. "We've been looking for a leader who is male. Soberano. But what if the kingpin of NX5 is female—Soberana? What if a woman is their leader and their goal is to never let us get to her. Like a beehive who protects their queen until death."

"Then the only woman who could be involved with Hank's case is—"

"Monica Hernandez." Judah scrolled on his phone, then flipped the display for Sasha to view. He'd pulled up the parking garage photo Sasha took at the crime scene. "What if she wasn't just the driver to help Coby get away, but instead, killed Hank. Coby did say he'd recognize Soberano's voice anywhere."

"That gives her means and opportunity. They played us. They knew during the WITSEC meeting they never planned to show up. They used the meeting to find out what we knew, buy some time and provide a chance for Monica to escape."

"Then NX5 didn't take them out. They've probably skipped across the border by now."

Judah scrolled on his phone again and tapped Nelson's number. Sasha's mind whirled with the danger Monica and Coby posed to her and Bodie if they remained free. She wasn't sure she'd ever be able to sleep soundly again. If the two criminals wanted to live a normal live and not face homicide charges, then she was the only one standing in their way of that freedom.

Chelsea texted Leila. "Monica's not pregnant, either.

According to Leila and her subpoenaed health records, she was never pregnant or in the ER. They threatened one of the nurses and her family to get her to lie for them."

"But why go to all that trouble?" Sasha fiddled with the deck of cards.

"Because they were there to set the bomb." Judah stood from his seat. "I need my laptop. Looks like our card game's over before it ever even started."

Flashes of the explosion swirled in Sasha's mind. She remembered the heat and the force that pushed her to the ground but little after that. If Monica was the one to set the bomb, then she'd stop at nothing to take Sasha off the prosecution's witness list if indicted. "DA Strut isn't even looking at Monica for Hank's murder."

"True, but he will after I talk with him. Our first priority is finding Monica and Coby. If we don't, then you and Bodie will never be safe."

Judah turned and walked into one of the bedrooms, closing the door behind him.

The fact he hadn't included himself in his last statement alarmed her. *You and Bodie will never be safe.* No mention of his safety or even being with them, wherever they ended up.

She prayed he found something concrete to bring the two fugitives in for good. If not, then she'd always be on the run, always looking over her shoulder, afraid someone might harm her child. WITSEC *was* the only option she and Bodie had.

Bodie would grow up without her sisters or his grandmother around. And what about Judah? She could never ask him to sacrifice his life for them, but at some point, he'd have to choose between being Bodie's father and being a cop. What she feared most was that he wouldn't choose her.

TEN

After twelve hours of research, five energy drinks and one sleepless night, Judah discovered Monica's location. Hank's files had proven to be the source of information he needed, taking him back to Monica's teenage years and where she grew up.

Once he called in a BOLO on her and targeted the area where she'd grown up, one of his patrol officers spotted her in Coventry Heights. This was not the kind of neighborhood cops liked to enter, and oftentimes they didn't exit, but in recent months a secret benefactor had begun to clean up the area. Crime dropped, and officers received fewer calls into the area to settle domestic disputes or calm down turf wars. Monica's presence in the area seemed to be beneficial to the locals—but the woman was a killer, and he wanted her to pay for taking his friend's life.

Judah was flipping through the documents from Hank's files on his computer screen when a knock rapped his door.

"Come in."

Sasha entered with scents of eggs, bacon and coffee following her. "Did you sleep at all last night?"

"Not really." He placed his laptop on the bed and took the plate she handed him, scarfing down a couple of bites. He turned his screen for her to see. "Take a look at this."

"Coventry Heights? What is this place?"

"This is where I think Monica and Coby are hiding."

"But this is miles east of Shadow Creek. Wouldn't they want to leave the country if they're wanted for murder?" Her finger pointed to Coby's known home in South America on the map.

"She's not been charged with anything yet. We didn't have enough proof against her, but I may have enough now. At least enough to get a search warrant."

He pulled up a few documents on his screen. "Hank was negotiating land deals with a company called West Haven Land Trust. It took me forever to find the connection, but Monica is the one running the company. She snatched up tons of property, built a large residence and has returned to the area hundreds of times since Hank closed the deal. Looks like she's building up an army of mercenaries to protect her."

"So Hank was in on helping a gang leader get ahead."

"Not on purpose. I don't think he knew she was running NX5, but when he figured it out, he tried to fire her as a client. That's most likely what got him killed. I found emails from him to Monica telling her she needed to find a new lawyer for her business needs."

"And we both know that once you help NX5—"

"There's no turning back unless you want to die. She killed him, Sasha. I feel it in my bones."

"But do those bones have evidence?"

"Nothing concrete. It's all circumstantial unless I can bring her in for questioning."

"Then I guess we need to bring her in. What do you need me to do?"

Judah snapped his laptop closed, slipped it into his backpack and grabbed his keys. "Stay here with Chelsea and Bodie, where I know you'll be safe."

"I'm a cop, too, Judah. I can't just sit by and let you go at this alone. You'll get yourself killed."

"Nelson and I will put a team together. He'll back me up." After a few more bites of scrambled eggs, Judah grabbed his cup of coffee and headed for the kitchen. Sasha followed and stopped beside the high chair where Bodie was finger-painting in his applesauce.

"I can be part of the team. I've helped with searches before."

He rinsed his plate in the sink. The last thing he wanted was for Sasha to be in harm's way. She was their target, and he would never be able to concentrate if she was involved. "It's too dangerous, and we need to make sure Bodie has one of his parents with him at all times."

"True. I'll stay with him, but you better come back to us. I mean it."

He stopped, turned off the water and pulled her into a hug, breathing in the sweet scent of her hair. "I'll come back. God willing."

She pulled back and looked up at him with searching eyes. He started to tell her about his time with God and Bodie last night, but he didn't want the moment to be rushed.

When Chelsea came out of her bedroom rubbing her eyes, Sasha stepped from his hold. "What's going on?"

"Judah knows Monica's location. He's going to head into a well-armed gang's territory, risk his life and arrest her."

"If you're going into armed NX5 territory, then you're going to need as many trained officers as possible. Since Shadow Creek is a small department, I can call in some reinforcements." Chelsea slathered butter on a piece of toast.

"We're not that small. At least we have a SWAT team but if you know some marshals who could help bring in two fugitives, that would be great. I'm hoping you'll stay here and protect Sasha and Bodie."

"Of course. I'm not leaving them alone."

Sasha scoffed. "Bodie and I will be fine. We have two other guards outside. Besides, you're going after Monica, and she's two towns over."

Chelsea put an arm around her sister's shoulders and squeezed. "You're stuck with me, sis. Don't worry, I've got a couple of friends who will keep Judah safe, plus you know Leila will be there. What do ya, say, Detective? Need a top-ranked sniper on your team? They can clear the area so your team can move on her residence."

"Yeah, that would be great. Have them meet us at the precinct."

Chelsea excused herself to make a few phone calls and brief her connections about the plan.

Bodie sat in the highchair, picking up pieces of egg and tossing them onto the floor. Judah placed a kiss on the top of Bodie's head, then turned to Sasha and slid his arms around her waist again. "Stay inside. Don't let anyone into this house. When I get back, we have a lot of things we need to discuss. Hopefully we can put all this behind us."

"I hope so." She gave him a hug. "Don't die. Bodie needs you."

"Only Bodie?"

She smiled. "Stay safe."

He didn't make any vows, knowing the bleak statistics about cops returning from a gang raid uninjured. He didn't want to make a promise he couldn't be sure he'd keep. If all went well, this would be over within a few hours, and then they could figure out their future together.

Judah pulled his pack onto his shoulder and stepped into the fresh morning. For the first time since his mom's death, he lifted his eyes to the heavens and hoped his new Savior would hear his prayer.

Rain pounded on the tin roof of the safe house, and Sasha stood at the window watching a young girl and her little brother playing on the back patio of the neighboring home. They drew with sidewalk chalk on the smooth surface each drawing their own pictures. Maybe one day Bodie would have a sibling and built-in playmate, like those two. The back door opened, returning Sasha to her current situation as Chelsea walked into the living area to check on her.

"Sasha, I don't mean to be a stick in the mud, but you need to step away from the windows. I can see you clear from the road, and if I can see you, then members of NX5 can see you. We don't want your location to be blown, and honestly, I'm not really in the mood for a gunfight today."

Sasha started to step away when the little girl waved at her. She smiled and returned the greeting, then released the curtain. "The only people who could see me were the kids next door. I don't think you're going to have to worry about them attacking me with a piece of sidewalk chalk. They're harmless."

"No one is harmless."

A loud crack of thunder boomed across the sky, ending in a child's screams. Sasha moved back to the window and saw the little boy was on the ground. The little girl was trying to move him back underneath the covered porch. "He's hurt."

Sasha raced toward the door, but Chelsea stepped in front of her. "Stay here. I'll go. You have your weapon, right?"

"In my bag."

"Keep it close while I walk over."

Sasha dug out her holster while Bodie was playing on the floor. She hated to wear her gun around her son, but if the situation required her to do so, then there was no other choice.

Sasha moved back to the window, but the children were gone. Chelsea was nowhere in sight, either.

Another clap of thunder boomed and vibrated the walls of the house, but Sasha heard another familiar noise. Two pops echoed across the yard. One of the officers stationed outside stumbled from around the corner of the neighbor's home and into view. His face was pale, and red stained the front of his shirt. He looked at her before dropping onto the soaked ground. Another man dressed in black stepped from the shadows.

They were here.

She flattened herself against the wall. *Bodie.*

The second officer rushed into the living area from the garage. "Get to the back bedroom and lock yourself inside. We've got trouble."

"Where's my sister?"

"She was walking the perimeter when a dark van pulled into the driveway, and they have her pinned. She can't get around them and back to the house without getting shot. We've called for backup, but someone jammed our signal and we couldn't get through to dispatch. You need to get in the bedroom now."

Sasha ran for Bodie and scooped him up in her arms, then raced to the main bedroom and locked the door. She reached into her pocket, but her phone wasn't there. She'd left it on the counter, and there were no other devices she could use to call for help. With a quick check of her weapon's magazine, she saw she had nine bullets. If there was only one intruder, she could take him out, but if there were more, she was in trouble.

She'd have to escape with Bodie. Get to the neighbor's house and find a way to call in the crime. She unlatched the window and kicked out the screen, ready for a quick exit. At least this house was only one floor. A row of bushes would camouflage her movements from any spotters who might be watching.

Heavy footsteps thudded on the porch out front, and Sasha waited. A loud bang echoed through the home, and more gunfire erupted inside the living area. She heard another body hit the floor. She feared the victim was the young guard assigned to keep her safe.

Tears pricked the corners of her eyes, but if she wanted to escape before the intruder found her, then she had to get out of here with her son. She was the only defense he had.

She heard a loud slam as one of the doors down the hall opened and hit the wall. They were checking the rooms. There was only one more before her location. Whoever Monica had sent to take her out was strong and methodical. Most likely military or former law enforcement.

She grabbed Bodie and moved to the window.

"Sasha Kane, I know you're in here."

She stilled at the male voice. His tone was familiar, recent.

"Why don't you come out so we can get the inevitable over? I can't have you testifying against me and ruining my life or career. Since Coby and Monica didn't finish the job, I guess I'm going to have to clean up their mess. Some things are just done better yourself."

DA Strut. She recognized his voice from the conference call when Coby and Monica were at the precinct. Had he been behind Hank's murder and the hit on her? With him being in the inner circle of police proceedings, that would explain how he'd been able to find the Whitmore property and now her safe house.

The next door slammed against the wall. She had to move before he entered. She pressed a finger to Bodie's lips, his eyes wide with fear, and carried him out the window.

Cold rain drenched them both upon their exit, and Bodie clung to her even tighter.

"Close your eyes, baby."

She prayed her son did as she said while she ran to the neighbor's home in search of a phone. The last thing she wanted was for Bodie to see the guard's dead body. She could've run in the opposite direction, but the neighbor's home was the closest shelter. If she could get inside, then she could dial 911 and swarm the house with sirens. That would keep Strut from carrying out his evil deeds.

Her only concern was for the family inside. If she entered and Strut followed, then she was putting their lives in danger, too, but she had no other choice. She prayed he didn't see her enter.

The grass was slick as she ran up the small hill and stepped through the unlocked screen door. She closed the glass behind her and tried not to drip all over the hardwood floors, but her clothes were soaked. Bodie's body shook against hers. He was cold.

"Hello? Is anyone home?"

A young woman rounded the corner into the kitchen. She seemed startled at Sasha's presence. "What are you doing? You can't come into my house without—"

"I'm so sorry for the intrusion, but we're in trouble. We were staying at the house next door, and some really bad people found us. You need to take your children and leave, but before you go, I need to call 911. Do you have a phone?"

The woman stood frozen for a moment, then rushed back through her home. "Izzy. Marcus. Come here."

Sasha moved away from the door in case Strut came looking for them. She closed the vertical blinds to further conceal her location. The woman returned with her purse, keys and the two children Sasha had seen outside in tow.

"Here. I brought you a blanket and phone. Your son looks cold."

Bodie had started to fuss, so Sasha took the cover and wrapped him in it. His body relaxed against her shoulder, and his shivers subsided.

"Are you sure someone's after you?"

"Positive, and they've already—" Sasha stopped her statement, not wanting to discuss the dead guard in front of the woman's children. "Take a look out the window."

The neighbor pulled back a curtain. "I see." She faced Sasha again. "Come with us. I've got a minivan and plenty of room."

Everything inside Sasha wanted to run with her, but she knew Strut would follow. "I can't put your lives at risk like that. It's best if you go and take your children with you."

"Well, I can't leave you inside my house to face a threat. Come on. We'll take our chances. I'm sure we can outrun them and get you to the police station. I'm not going to abandon you."

Sasha didn't have time to debate the matter, so she followed the woman down the dark hallway with her two kids close behind. The little girl, who couldn't be more than six years old, glanced back at her. "My name's Izzy, and that's my little brother, Marcus."

"I'm Sasha, and this is Bodie."

The woman opened the door into the garage and guided her kids toward the minivan. "Hop in and buckle up, Izzy."

She lifted her young son into the car seat and buckled him in. "I have a built-in car seat for your child. Will that work?"

"Of course. I'd rather have that than nothing."

The woman folded down the cushion, reached for Bodie and placed him in the seat. "I'll let you strap him in. I'm Donna, by the way."

"Nice to meet you." Sasha put Bodie in the chair and clicked the buckle. "I wish it wasn't like this."

"You and me both." She moved and rounded the car to the driver's seat.

Gunfire sounded from inside the house, and glass shattered. "Sasha?"

Strut's loud voice rang through the hallways and resonated through the garage door. Sasha hit the button to close the van's side door and slid into the passenger seat. "Did you lock up the house?"

Donna nodded and handed her a cell phone. "I don't think that's going to stop him, though. Here. Call 911."

"Hurry. It won't take him long once he hears the garage door go up."

Her new friend hit the button, and they waited for what felt like eternity. Loud thumps slammed against the interior door and Sasha looked in the side view mirror. The knob turned, and the only barrier keeping them safe vibrated with every hit from Strut or the person on the other side. As soon as the garage door raised enough, Donna hit the gas pedal and spun her tires peeling out of the driveway.

Strut ran out another side door and fired three bullets at the back of their vehicle, hitting the side. Sasha faced the kids. "Are y'all okay?"

Izzy's eyes were wide. "That was a bad man."

"Yes, he is, but he's gone now, and we're going to be okay." Sasha tightened the strap holding Bodie in his seat.

"I'm not so sure about that." Donna kept looking out her side rearview.

"Why? What's wrong?"

"Two things. He hit the gas tank and we have a leak."

"And the other?"

"We've got a tail."

Sasha looked up. A black van was gaining on them. "Does this thing go any faster?"

"Yeah. But we won't make it to the precinct. I'm losing gas fast."

Sasha dialed dispatch with the phone still in her hand. "This is Bravo-25. We have a 10-43 traveling east on Highway 64. Suspect is in a black van and is in pursuit of our burgundy Toyota Sienna. Suspect is identified as District Attorney Alex Strut. He is armed and dangerous. Need backup."

Dispatch alerted all units while Sasha scanned the area for some sort of exit or place to hide their vehicle before they ran out of gas. Donna rounded a curve, turned down a side road and whipped into a storage facility. She rolled down the window and typed in a code, opening the gate.

"Bravo-25. Dispatch. Can you provide your location so we can send units?"

"We just pulled into Edgetown Storage, off Oakland Drive. Our vehicle was losing fuel from a gunshot sustained to the gas tank. We're going to hide inside the facility."

The area was massive, with rows of indoor and outdoor storage units. Each aisle ran between at least five long warehouse-like structures placed end to end with about a three-foot distance separating the individual buildings. This allowed for workers to cross through to other aisles without having to traverse the entire length of the lot. Donna's building was labeled with a large white *M*, and the outside had seen better days but at least this would give them a good place to hide until police arrived.

"Here's my unit." Donna pulled to a stop. "I've had this rental unit for a while, but it doesn't have much in it. We can pull the van inside."

Sasha jumped out and opened the metal door. Other than a couple of shelving units and a large standing safe at the back, the space was pretty empty.

"What's in that?" She pointed at the large Winchester Ranger 28 long gun cabinet.

"My husband used to own a variety of Glocks, a couple of revolvers and a rifle. When we moved here, I had them put in storage."

"What do you mean 'used to own'? Are they still in there?" Sasha unbuckled her belt and reached for the door handle.

"He was killed in the line of duty last year and we moved back here to be near my family. He was a cop at the local precinct about two hours from here. I didn't like the guns in the house with my kids getting older. That's why I wanted to help you. He would've done the same."

The revelation stunned Sasha for a moment. "I'm so sorry. I didn't know."

"No time to worry about that now. We have to make sure these kids stay safe."

Sasha stepped from the vehicle. "That's why you are going to stay hidden here while I go check outside. Hopefully Strut went right on by."

"Sounds good. I'll keep an ear out for the cops. I still

have some connections with the department and can make some calls."

Sasha handed her the phone. "First, can you open the safe for me? I want to be armed in case I run into Strut."

The woman entered the combination and pulled open the door. Every weapon had been kept in meticulous condition. Sasha chose two Glocks and hid a knife in her boot. "Keep them quiet."

Sasha exited out a side door and kept to the shadows cast by the units. A few cars whizzed by on the road, and sirens pierced the air. For a moment her heart relaxed until she realized the sound was moving *away* from their location. The officers were headed in the wrong direction, even though she'd been clear about her location. She reached for the cell but had left the device with Donna and the kids.

The front entrance gate creaked and slid back. Sasha moved for a better view. She rounded the corner. Strut's black van pulled into the main aisle next to the office and inched along the asphalt. She followed, keeping a building between them, but when she came to the break between the structures, the van was nowhere in sight. Sasha gripped her gun tighter and traversed between the two buildings over to the main aisle for a better look. He must've gotten ahead of her or something.

She stepped around the corner. Hard metal pressed against her head. "Don't move and give me your gun."

Sasha raised her hands into the air, and he took her weapon, as well as her spare, but he didn't find the knife she'd hidden in her boot.

"You know, I wouldn't have found you if you hadn't called dispatch." He turned up the volume on a police radio, and chatter flooded from the speaker. "I pretended to be a cop and provided a sighting of this black van, but of course it was headed in the opposite direction from where you are now."

"They'll figure out our location and come back."

"Possibly, but by that time you'll be dead."

He shoved his gun into the back of her head again. "Now move."

Sasha faked a stumble and pulled out her hoop earring, dropping the piece on the ground. With all these units, there was no telling where she'd end up. Anything she could do would help officers find her. Strut grabbed her upper arm and moved her through the buildings faster, then stopped in front of one unit on the back row.

"You won't get away with this."

"Looks like I already have."

One of Strut's assistants who had been following behind pulled up the unit's door. Inside, a deep freezer sat against the back wall. He shoved her forward. "Get in."

Sasha figured he'd just put a bullet through her head, but dying of hypothermia was not the way she wanted to go. If she wanted to live, she'd have to fight her way out.

Judah walked through the residence belonging to Monica Hernandez and scoured every area for any hint as to where she'd gone. The neighborhood wasn't anything like he'd expected—it was nice, with playgrounds, community centers and a brand-new elementary school on the corner.

Leila searched through some of the drawers behind him. "Do you think she's listening in on our dispatch calls?"

"It's possible."

"Every time we plan a raid, seems like they always know we're coming. Like they're one step ahead."

"Maybe we have a mole in the department feeding her intel."

Judah pulled out his phone to message Sasha when he saw the notification from dispatch. "We need to get back to the safe house. The location's been breached, and two officers are down."

"That's not good."

His chest tensed. "Hurry."

Judah raced to the car with Leila on his heels and sped out of the area. "I never should've left her alone."

Leila had her phone pressed to her ear and typed on the laptop. "Any more information?" she asked, then paused and ended the call. "Units are on the scene. Sasha, the neighbor and the children are missing."

"Children?"

"Apparently, she ran next door for help. A mother and her two children were home. The minivan is gone. She's the wife of a fallen cop out of the Charlotte PD and seems to be trying to help them escape."

"Escape from who?"

"You're never going to believe it, but DA Alex Strut seems to be the one who killed the guards. Sasha called in and gave dispatch his identity. Said he was armed and dangerous."

"That's how he stayed one step ahead of us. He'd be able to get any information he needed about our locations. What about the guards?"

"Both dead."

"What about Chelsea? She's okay, right?"

"Other than beating herself up that this happened and a few bruises from a fight, she's okay and inside working to find her sister. I think she's called every marshal in the area."

He activated his blue lights and siren, hoping to move traffic out of his way. Within thirty minutes, he pulled into the safe house. Multiple officers blocked the road but flagged them on through. Crime scene investigators milled in and out of both houses. Judah parked and jumped from the car and met Nelson at the door. "What happened?"

"Once Strut had you and Leila out of the way with Monica's address, he made his move. A dispatch call came in from Sasha and we got units here, but she was already gone. We just got another call from dispatch to send units to Edgetown Storage. The area is huge, and I've called in more units to help. We don't know where they are, but Sasha was the one to call in the new location."

"How did we not know that Strut was our killer or worse, Soberano?"

Nelson shook his head. "He was able to manipulate the evidence and information we received to cover his tracks. We have security footage that shows him on camera killing our guards. We also have footage of him shooting at a burgundy minivan with Sasha in the passenger seat."

"What about Bodie? Was he in the van, too?"

"We don't have video footage of him but it seems most likely that the children are with them, since they aren't here."

Judah took a closer look. "What's Strut driving?"

"Dispatch sent out a BOLO for a black van, but then another officer came on the call with a visual of our suspect's vehicle headed past this location. I sent units after him, but when they caught up to the sighting location, the van was gone. I've reassigned them to Edgetown."

"Are Monica and Coby involved, too? Or any other NX5 members?"

"Not sure. We're looking at all suspects, but we discovered that Strut never filed their immunity papers with WITSEC. They must've taken off when they realized Strut planned to pin everything on them instead of setting them free."

Leila joined them. "Chelsea has a few more marshals headed to the storage facility to help with the search, along with the SWAT team."

"Then we'll head over there, too." Judah moved toward the garage door. "We have to get to Strut before he kills them."

Nelson stepped in his way. "You know protocol. You can't go in with us. Not with Bodie and Sasha being the victims."

"You need every man helping or we may not get to them in time. I need to be there when you find them. They're my family and I have to see that they're okay."

"Let's go, then."

Judah breathed a sigh of relief. He would lose his mind if he was blocked from helping find his family. He loved Sasha. She was his son's mother and the woman he never wanted to be away from again. He'd just gotten her back. With or without approval, Judah planned to be there— even if the move cost him his job. No one could keep him from saving his family.

He crossed the drive to his SUV. The entire trip, he white-knuckled the steering wheel and didn't even slow down when Chelsea grabbed for the door handle as he rounded the curves. He couldn't lose them. Not when he was this close to having everything he'd ever wanted.

Dear God. Please keep them safe. Don't take them from me. Not again.

ELEVEN

Sasha stared at the deep freezer's lid. Her time was running out, and if she didn't start fighting, Strut would make sure she never lived to see Bodie's third birthday. The man was stronger and had the advantage, but she still had a knife she could use. If only he didn't have a gun.

She faced him. "Wouldn't it be easier to just shoot me?"

Strut nodded to his gang member, and the man walked back to the door and pulled the metal barrier closed. "It would, but that would leave a blood trail, and things get messier that way. With you inside the freezer, even if the officers open this practically empty unit, they won't think to look inside. They take one glance around and move on to the next one. No one will find you in time."

He raised his gun. "Now, get in."

When she didn't move, Strut lunged for her, grabbed her hair and secured her in a chokehold, dragging her over to the freezer. She kicked her legs and planted her feet against the side. He squeezed her neck harder, but she was able to reach forward and grab her knife, then thrust the blade into his side.

Her body dropped to the floor, and her head bounced against the hard concrete. Sasha covered her head with her arms willing the instant shard of pain to go away.

Strut let expletives fly and stumbled around behind her. She looked up at him and pushed to her feet. He grabbed his side, applied pressure to the new wound and glared at her. Sasha held out the knife in front of her.

"Come at me again and I'll aim for your chest." Sirens drew closer, and blue lights flashed against the trees. "It's over, Strut. They've found you, and I'm not dead."

"Yet." His dark eyes narrowed, and he aimed his gun at her leg, then fired. Sasha screamed and grabbed the wound on her outer thigh. "Didn't anyone ever tell you not to bring a knife to a gunfight? By the way, my aim is impeccable. If you don't want another one, then you need to drop the knife and get in the freezer."

She straightened and placed the knife on the floor, praying the officers had heard the shot. However, with the piercing sirens still blaring, she was sure they hadn't. Strut charged toward her and put the barrel to her head. "Now."

Sasha shuffled backward, and Strut lifted the freezer lid. "Before I get in, why did you kill Hank? At least give me that if you're planning to leave me here."

"Stop stalling."

Sasha tried to fight him, but it was no use. He was too strong, and with one hard punch, she toppled over the side of the freezer and into the bottom. Before she could flip around to escape, the door came crashing down. Beating her fist against the lid was no use. Her death trap was sealed.

Judah's phone rang. An unknown number flashed across the screen, but he answered anyway. "My name is Donna O'Connell. He's got her. You have to hurry."

"How'd you get my number?"

"It's written on the inside of Bodie's blanket."

"You have my son?"

"I do. We're safe and inside unit 132."

"I'm two minutes out."

"You have to hurry. She went out to check on the man who followed us and never came back. I went to the door and peeked out. He had a gun aimed at her and took her back through the units away from the office. I think he's going to kill her."

Judah sat up straighter in the driver's seat and pressed the gas harder. "Are the other officers on-site?"

"I hear sirens and see some blue lights flashing through the trees, but I don't see any boots on the ground yet."

He had to keep Bodie safe. "Stay where you are and keep the children safe. I'll text your unit number to Sergeant Quinn. When cops come to your door, tell them everything you can remember."

"Will do."

By the time Judah arrived, Edgetown Storage was crawling with cops. According to Sergeant Quinn's text, they were searching every unit, but Sasha had not been found yet. They had found Donna, Bodie and the O'Connell children. Paramedics were checking them out inside the main office.

"Where are you going?" Leila cranked her neck as they drove by the doors. "Don't you want to go see Bodie?"

"Of course I do, but he's safe. Sasha isn't. The best thing I can do for my son right now is find his mother."

"But we need to check in at control to find out what they've searched and what's still left."

Judah continued to drive down the aisles. "That will take too long. If we start at the other side, we can meet them in the middle. That way will cover more ground."

"True, but—"

"If you were someone who took a hostage and knew the cops were coming through the main gate, where would you go?"

"I'd get as far away as possible."

"Exactly. He's got to be here somewhere, and my guess is that Strut will be back here. If we find him, that will put us closer to Sasha's location than anyone else." He slowed his vehicle and crept across the asphalt, looking between every building. Judah rolled down his window, listening for anything that might give him a clue to her exact location.

"We're at the last row. Let's get out and search. He's got her in one of these units, and there's at least a thousand on the premises. Do you have lock cutters?"

"In the back of the truck." Judah pointed. "There. Look."

Between the last two buildings, hidden against the tree line, sat a black van. "He's got her in one of these."

Judah stepped from the car, pulled his weapon and waited for Leila to grab the cutters. "Tell Quinn we need a K-9 unit back here."

Leila radioed the rest of the team while Judah slipped into the shadows between the buildings and walked toward the van. He kept his weapon aimed.

Movement to his left raced through the trees. *Strut.* Judah ran after him. "Police. Freeze."

Strut pivoted and aimed his weapon at Judah's head. "You'll never find her in time. There are too many units to check, and she'll be dead by the time you get to her."

"And if that's true, I'll make sure you pay."

Leila stepped from the shadows. "Give it up, Strut. You're surrounded."

"It'll be a cold day in Florida before I surrender."

Strut fired his weapon, and Judah lunged behind the van

for cover. The man ran to the driver's side, flung open the door and started the vehicle.

Red backup lights glowed in the darkness when Strut put the vehicle in Reverse. Judah jumped to the side to keep from being run over.

Four patrol cars wheeled around the suspect's vehicle, blue lights flashing, and officers surrounded him. Judah raced around to passenger side and slid the door open, aiming his weapon inside. Strut had moved to the rear and pulled the handle on the back doors.

Four officers greeted him with an official arrest slam to the ground and locked handcuffs around his wrists, then pulled him to his feet.

Judah got in his face. "Where is she, Strut?"

The disgraced district attorney smirked. "I want my lawyer."

Judah shoved him into the back seat of an officer's car and slammed the door closed.

"Cut off all these locks. Sasha's in here somewhere. When you find her, text me."

He prayed she was still alive, but Strut had a large lead on them. If he was already back at the van when they arrived, the outcome didn't hold much hope for Sasha. He had to find her. "I'll start at the other end. Nelson, you head to the other. Everyone else, spread out in between."

They moved quickly, but with every unit door he opened, his hopes sank. Thirty minutes passed like five, and still no Sasha. He had three numbers left in his section and no texts from anyone else displayed on his phone.

Judah cut the lock, raised the door and stepped inside the next unit. The air was cold, dank and moist. Nothing was inside but a deep freezer plugged in on the back wall. No junk piles to search through here. He figured if she was alive, he'd hear her yelling or making some kind of noise, but nothing yet. If the man had shot her, she wouldn't be able to call for help. Judah turned away to move to the next unit.

He snipped the next lock, combed through the mess, then scoured the last one. No sign of Sasha.

Static clicked on his radio. "We've been through them all—" Nelson's voice crackled "—and she's not here. He must've moved her or maybe she escaped."

"How?"

"He could've handed her off to someone else for an undisclosed location."

Judah ran a hand through his dark curls. He had to find her. If not for him, then for Bodie. "Were all your units filled to the rim with junk?"

"Every single one. I can't believe what some people keep. Disgusting."

Judah walked back to the almost-empty unit. This was the only one different. The only one with nothing inside. Not a piece of junk on a shelf or a tchotchke to sell. Only the hum of the freezer to lure him inside. Strut's words replayed in his head. *A cold day.*

Judah walked inside and flashed his light on the floor. A small puddle of blood was in front of the freezer. He crossed the empty space. "Meet me at number 542."

He flipped the outer latch holding the freezer closed and threw open the lid. His heart pounded.

Sasha was inside, curled into a fetal position in the corner. She looked as if she was sleeping—except for her blue lips and pale skin. He pulled her from the box, her body stiff and cold. She had no pulse or respirations. Nothing. He placed her body on the concrete and started CPR, compressing her chest in a rhythmic pattern. Nelson rounded the corner at a dead run, took in the scene and clicked his radio. "Get the paramedics in here now."

"Any idea how long she was in there?"

"Nope." Judah continued to press. "Come on, Sasha. Come back to me."

He couldn't lose her now. Not when he'd just gotten her back and connected with Bodie. They were supposed to be a family. The three of them together—somehow, some-way. Forever.

TWELVE

Lights flashed. Sirens blared. Warmth flowed through her body while footsteps slapped the floor around her. Bleach and antiseptic scents roused Sasha. She tried to open her eyes, but the glare was too bright.

"There's our girl." A blond-headed man in scrubs and a medical cap pressed a stethoscope to her chest and watched the monitors.

Someone took her hand. Strong heat flooded against her palm. "How's she doing?"

Judah.

How had he found her? The last thing she remembered was Strut forcing her into a deep freezer. As oxygen ran out and the cold invaded her body, she'd made her peace with death. She had Jesus now and He'd promised her eternal life. And Bodie had his father.

The blond man kept his eyes on the vital signs. "We thought we were going to have to do a thoracic lavage, but it looks like her core temperature is coming up. She's at thirty-six degrees Celsius." He turned to a nurse. "Give her two more liters of warmed saline and fifty mics of epi, then send her on to the ICU so they can continue monitoring her."

"Is family allowed in the ICU? Her mother and sisters are on their way," Judah said.

"Two at a time. They shouldn't keep her in there long if she continues to improve, but for the next twenty-four hours, I want her monitored. After she returns home, she'll need several weeks to recover. She's blessed to be alive, and I'd say that has a lot to do with you."

Bodie. She couldn't make her tongue work to ask him about Bodie.

Judah squeezed her hand. "I'm blessed to still have her. My son and I don't want to live without her."

"Good news. I think she'll make a full recovery, but we'll know more tomorrow."

Fatigue overtook Sasha, and she closed her eyes again.

Judah agreed to stay at the farmhouse with Bodie while Sasha's mother and sisters spent every waking minute at the hospital. He'd spent a few hours by her side, too, but Sasha wanted him to care for their son until she was discharged. She'd improved quickly once they got her warmed up and monitored overnight. This morning she'd called and said the doctor planned to release her. He wanted everything to be perfect when she arrived at the farmhouse.

Judah had washed the dishes, made her favorite magic cookie bars and brewed a pot of coffee before he received a text at 1:00 p.m. that they were on their way.

"More ju." Bodie sat beside him on a stool and splashed in the sink. Most of the suds were on the floor, and Judah made a note to clean that up before she came home, too.

"You've made a mess, buddy. How about we rinse off, clean up the floor and then go draw a picture for when Momma comes home."

"Okay. Momma home?"

"Yes. Today. In fact, she should be on her way now."

The little boy clapped his hands together, sending bubbles into the air. Judah helped him climb down, then gave him a towel to wipe up the floor while he used a mop. These last few days had been the highlight of Judah's life. He'd never dreamed being a father would be so fun, exhausting and satisfying all at the same time. He wouldn't trade a minute of it for any part of his former life.

"Your clothes are soaked—" he sniffed the air and got a whiff of another unpleasant smell "—and stinky. We can't have you stinking when your momma gets home." Bodie wiggled down and toddled to the stairs, toward where his clean diapers and clothes were in the bedroom.

After Judah changed him, they returned to straighten up the living room. Bodie pulled out crayons and paper from the television cabinet, then placed them on the coffee table. "Draw picture."

Judah finished straightening the couch pillows and took a seat on the floor. Bodie climbed up in his lap and pointed to the blank sheet. "Momma."

Judah drew the best stick figure with long dark hair that he could. Bodie pressed his finger to the paper again. "Me. Hold hands with Momma."

Judah was no artist, but his son didn't seem to mind. He tapped the space next to him. "You. Hold hands with me."

He'd dreamed of this moment with his son from the first time he saw him. God had given him a second chance to make a fresh start, to become a new person, and he wasn't going to waste it. Judah added muscles onto his stick arms, making Bodie laugh. Then he added a word at the top. One that encompassed his new life and faith.

Someone rapped a knock on the door and pushed it open. Sasha, wheeled by her mother in a chair, fussed. "You know I can walk, right?"

"We're taking a few extra precautions until you're one hundred percent better."

"But—"

"No buts. I'm your mother, and this is how things are going to go for a while."

Bodie toddled over to Sasha as fast as his legs would go and climbed up in her lap. She wrapped her arms around him and smothered his cheeks in kisses. "I've missed you so much. Have you been a good boy?"

She looked up at Judah when the little boy climbed down again, crossed the room and carried the picture back to her. She smiled and took the picture from her son, then met Judah's gaze again. Tears glistened in her eyes.

"Welcome home," he said and shoved his hands in his pockets, hiding a sudden rush of nerves. He loved her, but they hadn't discussed their future since before she was in the hospital.

"I'll go put your things away." Her mother pushed Sasha's suitcase handle down and lifted the bag, then headed up the stairs. Judah was thankful to have a moment or two alone with her and Bodie.

Sasha stood and shuffled to the couch, the picture still in hand. Bodie climbed up beside her and pointed to the word Judah had written across the top. "Read."

"The word is *family*." She lifted her gaze to his but didn't say any more. He wasn't sure if she was angry for exposing Bodie to a concept she wasn't ready for or happy that he was ready to move forward. The woman had the face of a cardplayer.

Judah took a seat beside her. "Bodie wanted the three of us in the picture. I hope that's okay." He reached for the corner of the paper. "If not, I can throw it away."

Her hand fell on top of his. "I love the drawing. Although I can't help but wonder if you're sure you're ready? This is a serious, life-altering decision, and I don't want you to feel pushed into anything."

"I've never been more serious about anything in my life."

She pulled her hand from his and twisted her hair into a loose bun. A dark tendril fell loose against her cheek. "And what about God? I won't go back to a life without Him as the foundation of our family."

"Remember the night at the safe house when I spent time with Bodie? That wasn't the only reason I wanted some time alone. I prayed that night." He fought back the burn of tears in his eyes. "Me and God are good, and I'm ready to be part of this family, in more ways than one."

The corners of her eyes lifted. "Really? I thought after your mom—"

"Death is a part of life, and even though my mom didn't live the best life, in the end she changed. I know my mom is with God in heaven. I want to make sure I see her again. Even in the dark times, God is still good, and I see that now."

Bodie wiggled off the couch to play with his trucks on the floor, and Sasha moved closer, slipping her fingers back into his. "What changed your mind?"

"Bodie. The overwhelming love I feel for him made me realize that God's love for me is so much more. I'd do anything for Bodie, provide for him, protect him, give my life for him…and you. God did the same for me. Gave up His only son for me, even when I turned my back on him. My mother's death hurt, but you and Bodie have shown me God's love and forgiveness."

Judah reached up and twisted the dark tendril and brushed her cheek with his fingers. "I love you, Sasha. I always have and always will."

He leaned forward and brushed his lips against hers—tender and longing, ready to seal the bond he never wanted to break. "Will you give me another chance? I'm so sorry for before. I want you and Bodie as my family."

He pressed his forehead against hers and waited, breathing in the honey scent of her hair, praying she wouldn't refuse him again. He didn't think his heart could take another rejection.

Her thumb ran across his fingers, and she moved closer, giving him another kiss. "On one condition."

He leaned back and met her gaze. "Anything."

She held up the picture he'd drawn. "You have to learn how to draw a proper stick figure, because this one needs some work."

Judah snatched the drawing from her fingers and leaned in for another kiss, but then a bright flash interrupted the moment. They both looked at their son.

Bodie held Sasha's phone and clicked another photo before crawling up between them. "Look."

Taking the device from her son's hands, Sasha flipped the camera around for a group selfie. "How about one with all three of us?"

Bodie clapped his hands and snuggled into Judah's lap. Another God-given dream come true.

EPILOGUE

One year later

The sun warmed Sasha's bedroom in the renovated farm-house situated amid the fall colors lining the base of her mountain view. She lifted the window and breathed in the crisp air.

Sasha never thought she'd be here, living on the acreage she and Judah had bought together. Two weeks ago, she and Bodie had moved in while Judah stayed in his own place. They'd barely seen each other before the wedding with all that needed doing before their special day.

The bedroom door creaked behind her.

"Are you ready to put on your dress?" Her mother entered first, followed by her four sisters.

Sasha crossed the room and fingered the lace on the white gown. "I've never been more ready for anything in my life."

Toddler footsteps slapped the floor, and a rosy-cheeked Bodie ran in, covered in mud. "Momma, look what I found."

He held up his hands, and a wiggly frog fought for his release. "Where did you get that?"

"Dad and I went to the creek."

A soft knock landed against the door. "I'm not coming

in—" Judah's voice echoed into the room "—but if you could send Bodie out to me, I'll get him cleaned up and ready for the day."

Dani steered Bodie and his frog back toward the door. "I've got this, Sasha. Don't worry. I'll make sure he's ready."

"Thanks."

Her sister closed the door behind her and Sasha could hear her scolding Judah for letting Bodie get all dirty just an hour before the wedding.

"At least he didn't have his tux on yet." Her mother lifted the hanger from the hook and removed the dress. "You're going to make a beautiful bride. Isn't she, Leila?"

Her sister crossed the room to where Sasha stood. "She is. But I'm still mad at you for pairing me up with TJ. What were you thinking, Sasha? He's my ex."

"Just wait until I toss you my bouquet. You're next, you know. He's one of Judah's best friends, and call me silly, but I think you two are good together."

"You weren't even here when we dated."

"True. But he did save my life at the diner. That should count for something. A man like that should be given a second chance."

Leila rolled her eyes and helped Sasha slide into the dress while their mother adjusted the fabric.

"Simply beautiful." Holly fluffed the long train. "I love how the lace has a subtle sparkle when the light hits it. And the open back is gorgeous."

Sasha turned and looked at herself in the mirror. Tears burned the corners of her eyes. "I never thought this day would come, or that Judah and I would be together again."

Chelsea handed her a tissue. "Don't you cry. Not yet,

anyway. You'll ruin your makeup, and I spent an hour making your face perfect."

She dabbed the corners of her eyes. "Okay. I'm good."

Sasha moved to the window and looked down on the flat area of grass that ran by the river. A white arch had been erected next to the creek that glimmered in the sunlight. White chairs decorated with corresponding bows sat in perfect alignment. The guest list was small, but that's how she and Judah wanted their special day—surrounded only by family and friends.

When the time came for the ceremony to begin, Sergeant Quinn met her at the bottom of the stairs. "Wow. Judah is one blessed man."

"Thanks for walking me down the aisle."

"I'm honored to do so. Your father was one of my best friends, and I learned more from him than anyone about our jobs."

Sasha slipped her arm into the crook of his elbow. "Before we go out there—" She paused.

"Yeah?"

"Strut's trial's coming up next week. We are going to get a conviction, right?"

He placed a hand over hers. "We've done some of our best work and have collected mountains of evidence against him. Looks like Strut has been Soberano ever since Coby's brother was shanked in prison. Strut worked for the man and didn't bring many charges against him or the gang. They were good friends but when he was killed, it left a void to be filled. Strut got greedy and we have the financial records to prove it. Now, the prosecutor needs to make sure she sends him to prison."

"And what about Monica and Coby?"

"They were apprehended when they crossed the border

and will be extradited in a couple of weeks." He gave her hand a pat. "This is your wedding day, and these are the last people you should be thinking about."

"I know. But after everything we went through last year, I guess I still want to make sure Bodie and I are safe."

As if on cue, her son ran from the kitchen with chocolate on his face and her sister Dani chasing after him. "Come here, Bodie."

Sergeant Quinn stopped her son before his chocolaty fingers landed on Sasha's dress. Her son reached out for her, but Quinn held him back. "Momma."

"Let Dani clean you up and then you can hug me. We want to make sure my dress stays nice and white."

Bodie looked at his fingers and stopped fighting, then let Dani wipe off his hands with the cloth she held. Sasha crouched down and gave her son a hug. "I love you, little man."

"Love you. Are you marrying Daddy?"

"I am. Are you ready to be a family?"

A smile filled her son's face, and he nodded.

Wedding music started to play, and Sasha's sisters proceeded out the door while Bodie escorted her mother to her seat and then stood beside Judah. Bells rang three times, and the doors opened.

Judah stood at the end of the aisle, dressed in his black tux with a white bow tie. She'd never loved another man like she loved Judah Walker. He met her gaze, and loved filled her soul as she stepped forward. Bodie reached up for his father's hand. This was her family. Her gift from God. Her stick-figure drawing. Forever.

* * * * *

Dear Reader,

Sometimes when writing a story, the words just won't come. Authors can get stuck or bogged down in the quagmire of our plot, unable to pull ourselves out, but that is when we turn to our amazing editors, who always make our stories better. I want to give a shout-out to Besarta Sinanovic and all the Love Inspired Suspense editors who work so hard and diligently to make everything we write sound amazing. If it were not for them, we truly would be without words. We appreciate those who brave the quicksand, extend us a limb and pull us into a glorious story. Thank you!

Blessings,
Shannon Redmon